ALTERDO'S AXIOM:

"To identical stars, similar planets and comparable histories."

Alterdo's cyclical view of history had received its initial confirmation. The planet Noldaz, like the ancient Earth, was to have a heroine who would save her countrymen from the domination of their enemies. If everything happened as it should, Liane would eventually liberate the country's capital and have her king crowned.

Tiadann, who disputed Alterdo's theory, commented: "This young peasant girl is apparently about to become a new Joan of Arc. The kingdom, at war for so many years, needs a hero around whom to rally. A man would have done just as well. Nevertheless I do not consider my views wrong. The slightest incident may completely change the mission of our warrior Maid. I guarantee that if she were to disappear, the history of Noldaz would make no further mention of her."

"We shall see," replied the cosmic historian.

THE JOAN-OF-ARC REPLAY

by

Pierre Barbet

Translated by
STANLEY HOCHMAN

DAW BOOKS, INC.
DONALD A. WOLLHEIM, PUBLISHER

1301 Avenue of the Americas
New York, N. Y. 10019

Translated by Stanley Hochman

Cover art by Karel Thole.

FIRST PRINTING, APRIL 1978

1 2 3 4 5 6 7 8 9

PRINTED IN U.S.A.

Prologue

Liane wandered aimlessly in the family garden. She was enjoying the warm caress of the sun on her bare arms and listening to the melodic trills of the birds hidden in the foliage. In the distance, on the side of a hill, she could see her parents bent over the soil. Gruff peasants, they worked hard to wring a livelihood from their small but fertile plot of land; there were five children to be fed.

As you can see, Noldaz is a planet just like the old Earth. Only its position at the galactic antipodes had thus far protected it from being meddled with by the Lactean Empire, which ruled over almost all the planets of the Milky Way. Her sun, the color of old gold, lights up a slightly bluish-mauve sky. Nature at her most abundant offers her riches to the peoples of a still medieval civilization. But alas, an interminable war is ravaging Lonk, one of the proudest kingdoms on the planet, and the country's peasants suffer cruelly.

Heedless of these troubles, the young girl was reeling off a joyous song. Suddenly, on her right, a blazing light illuminated the sky over the church. The blinding brightness made her tremble. Yet the phenomenon was not new to her; this was the third time she was witnessing it. On the first occasion she had doubted her sanity. The second vision had frightened her badly, even though the voice she heard was gentle and persuasive: a child of twelve is unaccustomed to such marvels.

This time Liane was less stupefied when, squinting her eyes, she saw a majestic figure splashed with golden flames, its hands resting on the pommel of a blazing sword. There could be no doubt; it was the Archangel Lignel himself, just as she had often admired him in illuminated books of devotion. Lignel: the mystical defender of her ravaged country, the all-powerful seraphim, captain of Heaven's armies.

"*Liane, Liane, be good and pious because you are destined to accomplish great things!*" the shining vision repeated several times.

Fascinated, the little girl slowly bent her head in sign of submission. Her gaze had caught dazzling angelic legions hovering around the winged giant. Then the vision slowly faded. Liane sank to her knees, and for a long time remained that way, meditating over what she had just heard . . . How could a poor thing like herself accomplish miracles? She, who couldn't even read or write! Her meager household skills were barely enough to allow her to help her mother. Sometimes she would guard her father's lambs but she didn't like to because she was afraid to remain alone in the fields. A gang of ruffians might at any moment suddenly spring from nowhere.

At sowing time she would sort the seeds before her father planted them in the fertile earth. When it was time for the harvest, she shared the anguish of her parents, who were constantly afraid lest a horde of pillagers seize the crop. Occasionally, she helped transport the sacks of golden grain, with the result that she was as muscled as a lad. Then it would be autumn and soon winter. The monotonous days stretched endlessly in the humid and glacial stone house. After she had finished with her spinning or weaving, she would make bread or bring the animals their fodder. Then the sun would return, and the monotonous cycle of the seasons would begin all over again.

Nothing about Liane or her life distinguished her from the other girls in the region. In the springtime, she danced and sang with the young people of the village under the magic tree hung with garlands of flowers. This was the way the peasants paid homage to the spirits of the woods and fields—the fairies in which they really ought not to have believed but who were nevertheless greatly feared by all, so it was just as well to remain in their good graces!

At night vigils and wakes, the old people would often recount the ancient legends. According to one of these tales, the kingdom of Lonk, which had been lost by a woman, the perfidious Queen Usmane, would be liberated from the Incl occupiers by a maid. Liane would be enraptured, but the mad thought that she might be the chosen one never even occurred to her.

For more than a century now, the king of the Incls had been fighting to gain the crown of the king of Lonk. His well-trained armies had won many victories, which they owed in part to an ultimate weapon: the crossbow, which could completely pierce the armor of the Lonkian knights.

A peace treaty had ceded half of Lonk to the enemy. The king's daughter—dishonor, boundless dishonor!—had wed the shameless Incl king, thus bringing to her son Dronz the succession of her parents' kingdom. Worse yet, the Duke of Xovia, whose fief bounded the southern frontier of the sweet kingdom of Lonk, allied himself to Dronz, and his troops began to ravage the countryside.

The poor dauphin Sranz, legitimate heir to the throne of Lonk, saw himself dispossessed of his crown by the Treaty of Oyes and lost all hope of recovering it by force of arms. In every season, bands of brigands, pillagers of all kinds, put the country to fire and the sword.

To protect themselves, Liane's father and his friends had restored the ancient fortification that rose above the banks of the nearby river. As soon as sentinels sounded the alarm, young and old would race to this refuge, taking their wretched belongings with them. In fortified chateaus here and there, some Lonkian nobles also continued the struggle, and in addition, several cities still held out against the Incl artillery.

Determined to settle the matter once and for all, the young king of the Incls sent a powerful host across the sea, and in this year of grace 1428 the situation of the Lonks seemed desperate. Without an army, without money, without courage, all the dauphin could do was call upon heaven to throw back the legions that were pouring over the channel to be in on the death.

And it was then that Liane's celestial voices became urgent: "*Daughter of God, why do you tarry?*" they repeated endlessly. "*The wretchedness of the kingdom is great! Leave your father, your mother, your village and your friends. Go to the aid of your king . . .*"

It was no use for the maid to weep bitter tears and object: "How can a simple peasant girl make war?"

The voices became imperative.

"*Take up the banner of the King of Heaven! Bran-*

dish it with faith and courage: God will come to your aid! Go to Captain Luvic d'Orselle, who governs the town of Irmorie. He will give you a knightly escort to the palace of the dauphin. You will order Sranz to raise the siege of Fnar and then you will lead him to the holy city of Irnu, where he will be anointed king just as his ancestors were. After that—I tell you truly—you will drive the Incls from your country!"

Anguished and torn, Liane ended by submitting to her celestial voices. One morning she left her native village, the home of her parents where she had spent her childhood. The maid went off to visit a cousin, a man of good sense who lived nearby. This departure by no means pleased her father: how could a young girl abandon her home to wander the roads? But Liane had been able to depict the great misery of the kingdom in words so heartbreaking, and she seemed to have so much faith in her mission, that the simple man was shaken.

The cousin too had been unenthusiastic. But Liane reminded him at great length of the prophecy that a maid would save the kingdom, a prophecy delivered to the Incls by the disloyal Queen Usmane at the time of the Treaty of Oyes. She nevertheless guarded her secret and limited herself to emphasizing that if no one appeared to give the gentle dauphin new courage, the Incls would eventually occupy the entire kingdom of Lonk.

After long delays the good man allowed himself to be convinced: Liane's family had always supported the royal family. He therefore agreed to escort his young relative to the city of Irmorie, whose garrison was commanded by Luvic d'Orselle, loyal servant of the Duke of Fnar, uncle of the Dauphin.

The sweet month of May was at its most seductive as the maid rode across hill and dale, heading south. Could she in any way have suspected the drama through which she was to live?

Chapter One

Far away, in the Imperial Lactean city at the antipodes of the Milky Way, two learned men—Iern'an, who held the chair in galactic history, and young Celsar, his favorite assistant—were having a heated discussion.

At ease in a condition of bluish stasis, their brains, encased in spherical containers, pulsed like luminescent globes. Fine reticles similar to neurons glowed within the shining plasma, while protuberances like glial cells brought the energy substances necessary to the sound functioning of their psychic faculties.

The professor, whose temperament was rather conservative, was listening in amusement to the nonconformist theories of his student. He seemed to recognize in Celsar himself when he had been some five hundred years younger—decisive, impulsive, convinced that he had latched onto the supreme truth. In short, he found the fiery enthusiasm of his disciple quite sympathetic.

"I've always held that throughout the Galaxy the great metaphysical and historical themes turn up periodically in cases of ethnic similarity," expounded the professor. "I might even add that there is a striking resemblance between certain planets. In other words, the unfolding of history is cyclical. The ancient

Earthlings knew this from time immemorial. . . . Think of the Greeks, of Engels, of that Belgian historian Henri Pirenne."

"I don't contest that point. According to your lapidary formula: 'To identical stars, similar planets and comparable histories.' But what I cannot accept, dear friend, is your insistence that this evolution—for example, from a theocracy to an enlightened republic—is the same without exception!"

"Careful now, my good Celsar! Don't carry what I said to an extreme. . . . Of course local divergencies may show up in the details, but in the main, the schemas found will always be identical."

"Even if expert historians were to intervene?"

"Of course! In the long run, after a few divergencies, events would lead to a similar end."

"Not true, not true! I maintain that specialists such as ourselves could profoundly modify an historical schema."

"In points of detail. Not in ultimate results."

"I'm sorry but I must contradict you, in spite of my great respect for you: every event in history is a particular case, and the repetitions that have been observed are not inevitable. I'm convinced that I can completely modify the historical development of any planet I choose!"

Iern'an began to warm to the game. Regardless of his friendship for his young colleague, he could not accept such contradiction without reacting.

"Well, I can see only one way to settle our dispute!" he exclaimed. "Let's choose a planet in a particular situation and we'll see what you can do. On condition, of course, that you bring your influence to bear only on relatively minor factors. You know that we are absolutely forbidden to make any important modifications in the normal development of events on the primitive planets that we study."

"Agreed. . . . You can stop me whenever you've become convinced of your error. There's nothing like the experimental method! Now, all we have to do is choose the subject of our investigation."

"So as to be sure not to prejudice the results, I won't insist on a subject of my choosing. We'll just draw a number at random and turn it over to the general encyclopedic memory of the Empire. Agreed?"

"That seems fair enough to me. Let's begin . . ."

The two started a complex series of maneuvers that more or less corresponded to a throw of the dice.

"Three hundred and two thousand, four hundred and three," noted the professor. "Fine. Let's see what the computer memory bank has to say about this number."

"Planet Earth, the case of Joan of Arc . . ."

"Now that's a fascinating subject of study! I couldn't have suggested anything better. Let's see—what planet in the galaxy is now experiencing events similar to those that happened on Earth after 1412?"

The two historians once more questioned the encyclopedic memory bank, which immediately furnished the required information.

"Planet Noldaz, star Sigma 32," said the assistant. "This promises to be exciting! Let's see. . . . We'll be dealing with mammalian bipeds of two sexes who have a carbonaceous metabolism, live in temperate zones, and breathe oxygen. That makes for a great similarity with the ancient Earthlings, the only difference being that these creatures have only four toes and a cutaneous pigmentation that tends toward mauve . . ."

"A typical and very classic case in our galaxy,

where carbonaceous biologies are legion. We will assume their form, assimilate their language, and start off for this planet immediately. The journey will be fairly rapid. And now, my friend, goodbye for the present, and may the best man win!"

The preparations of the two scholars were soon complete, since the University had vast means at its disposal and enjoyed complete autonomy of action. Upon a simple request from the professor, a hypersphere transport was placed at their disposition and loaded with all necessary supplies and materials while the synthesizers were giving the Lacteans a human morphology. When they saw each other again aboard the vehicle, their strange disguises made them laugh like schoolboys.

The spaceship had been programmed in advance and did not have to be piloted. It knew the shortcuts through seven-dimensional space, took advantage of the sling effect of the dwarf stars, and avoided spatial-temporal turbulence.

Iern'an and Celsar were free to spend their time perfecting their knowledge of the medieval language and choosing a fabricated identity that would allow them to move about freely on this planet torn by continuous warfare.

The professor took the disguise of an astrologer and baptized himself Alterdo Zanzini; his colleague remained his assistant under the pseudonym Tiadann Remt. By assuming these roles, they were able to disguise among their trumpery equipment the various scientific instruments that were absolutely indispensable to their mission. The only thing left to determine was the place and the time of their landing. By common consent they chose the kingdom of Lonk and the city of Irmorie, in which, according to their computers, a young heroine would soon make her appearance. The hypersphere therefore quietly set them down near the city they had chosen and then regained altitude and placed itself in a waiting position in a synchronous orbit.

Though the appearance of Irmorie was confusing to the scholars, Tiadann was ecstatic. The houses with their thatched or red-tiled roofs, the simple lifestyles of the inhabitants, the wood fires over which sides of venison were roasted to a golden brown, the motley costumes, the shining armor of the soldiers—everything completely enchanted the young savant, who was excited by this opportunity for close study of a primitive civilization.

Thanks to the gold pieces that filled the moneybags that hung from their belts, the pseudo-astrologers were able to treat themselves to a reasonably comfortable room in the town's best inn. No financial problems for them! Their spaceship's synthesizer furnished them with as many coins as they wanted by copying the models Alterdo had obtained in exchange for a small diamond.

The outgoing qualities of the astrologer, his generosity, the tricks he willingly performed in the inn's smoky-ceiling, beamed dining room, all soon made him very popular. Merchants and peasants alike were astonished at the accuracy of his horoscopes: this magician seemed able to read their most secret thoughts.

Luvic d'Orselle, the castellan of the fortified manor, liked to live well. He enthusiastically welcomed these magi whose skills he had heard much of, and since he favored the dauphin's cause, he took the opportunity to question the astrologers about the future of Lonk.

Alterdo found himself in an embarrassing situation: if the course of history unfolded normally, the captain would soon be visited by Liane, and the professor did not want to interfere with events by adding the weight of his authority to the young girl's story. Nevertheless, he had to support his reputation as a soothsayer by giving proof of his skill.

Finally, the astrologer decided on a prudent compromise: "The years to come," he told his host, "will be rich in events favorable to him in whom you are so interested. In addition, you will soon receive an unexpected visit . . ."

Though this was rather vague, the captain seemed satisfied. He gave the two friends access to him whenever they desired, and this was exactly what the pseudo-astrologers wanted. And so it was Alterdo and Tiadann were present when Liane of Erck, now fifteen years old, made her appearance in the great hall where Luvic d'Orselle sat surrounded by soldiers and burghers.

The Maid was modestly dressed: a beige camisole over a patched red skirt. Her long brown hair was held back by a scarlet foulard, from under which several curls escaped to frame her face. Her cheeks were flushed, and the charm of her harmonious features was heightened by the exaltation she felt; everybody present was immediately won over by her youth, her ardor, and the faith that animated her. With a rapid glance she took in all the notables and unhesitatingly strode toward the captain of the fortress, who was undoubtedly completely unprepared for what this poor young peasant girl was calmly about to say.

"Luvic d'Orselle, I have been sent to you by Our Lord so that you can dispatch word to the gentle dauphin to stand firm, but not to summon his enemies into battle at this time. Before long, the Lord will send him help . . ."

Astonished, the captain stared at the young girl and asked, "Who has told you so?"

"The King of Heaven. In truth, the kingdom of Lonk belongs to God and not to the dauphin. Nevertheless, Our Lord wishes Sranz to become king and rule over Lonk in spite of the Incls who accuse him of being a bastard. He *will* be king, and *I* want to lead him to his coronation . . ."

After a moment of stupefaction, the gruff captain reacted with brutal decisiveness. "This maid is clearly out of her mind!" he roared. "Have her sent back to her parents immediately. A good thrashing from them should make her see reason. Has a maid ever before been involved in politics?"

In a corner of the hall, Tiadann smiled and whispered to his companion, "Well, what do you have to say about this? From all appearances, it doesn't seem that events will follow the course you expected!"

"Patience," replied the professor, "first attempts are rarely crowned with success. Heroines such as this do not let themselves be rejected so easily . . ."

A few days passed. Alterdo kept a scrupulous record of events. Messengers brought word of Incl victories over the troops of the sickly dauphin. They also reported that the Incls had just laid siege to Fnar, one of the few cities still under the control of the Lonks.

Sranz had made no attempt to interfere, but luckily the city had sufficient supplies to enable it to hold out for quite some time. Besides, the Incls, convinced in advance of the outcome of the fight, were in no particular hurry. No effort was made to launch an assault, and the Lonks contented themselves with building fortifications around Fnar in order to isolate it and prevent supplies from getting through.

In Irmorie meanwhile, the two Extraterrestrials, comfortably installed in the inn, were savoring Lonkian cuisine, without doubt one of the tastiest in the universe. The two discovered that the Noldazians had various talents that the observation satellites had never reported on; their eyes, for instance, were sensitive to polarized light. During daylight hours, they could orient themselves with extreme precision because the sky as they saw it did not have the same color in one direction as it did in another. As a result, the Lonkian painters were able to create marvelous pictures whose great variety of tones surpassed in beauty the works generally turned out by humans.

In addition, both the Lonks and the Incls were endowed with an extremely sensitive sense of smell, which made them great fanciers of perfumes. Merchants of the southern cities, the Xovians in particular, would search far beyond the seas for the aromatic drugs and spices that the Noldazians set great store by. The Duke of Xovia owed a great part of his wealth to the trade in this merchandise.

Accumulating documents and records that would be of the greatest interest to their colleagues, the two scholars compiled a detailed study of the local civilization. Their conversations with Irmorie's notables also enlightened them on the political situation of the country. Noldazians, they learned, were completely devoid of national feelings. The peasants were indifferent as to whether they were exploited by the Incls or the Lonks: it had no effect on their daily problems. Though they were often extremely attached to the person of the sovereign—some being for Sranz's dynasty and others for Dronz's—what they wanted above all was a lasting peace. The Incls were only intent upon establishing a single monarchy, which would unite the Lonk throne with their own; they had already named a regent in the person of Rog Bacdir, because their king, still very young, was not old enough to be crowned. To accomplish this unification they reverted to a method formerly used by a Lonkian duke who had united the island of the Incls with his domain of Ronande, which was situated on the continent. The fact was, the Treaty of Oyes had purely and simply delivered the Lonkian crown to the young sovereign Dronz VI, who had received it as his inheritance from his mother. Tiadann pondered this information because he wanted to use it in effecting a radical modification of events on Noldaz.

Meanwhile, Liane had not left the city; she was awaiting her hour. Many people came to see her out of curiosity, and she had become known as the Maid of Fnar. . . . Soon she made another attempt to carry out her mission, and on a cold winter morning once more presented herself to the worthy Lovic d'Orselle.

The young girl was still dressed in the same skirt of coarse cloth, and she again demonstrated the same assurance. "My heavenly voices have ordered me to return to see you, sir," she announced in a firm voice. "You must take me to the dauphin. He will place soldiers under my command and I will raise the Incl siege of Fnar. By Heaven, you, a faithful vassal of the Duke of Fnar, cannot refuse me! Afterward, I will lead the gentle dauphin to the city of Irnu, because he is more than old enough to be anointed king, like all his ancestors!"

This time the lord of the manor did not send her away. Still hesitant, however, he had the young peasant girl examined by a priest in order to assure himself that he was not dealing with a witch of some kind. Rites of purification were performed over the young girl and the Sire d'Orselle was given assurances: the Maid was a true believer.

At the same time, reports of new disasters came from Fnar: a convoy bringing food to the besieged had been intercepted. If the city did not receive immediate help, it would surely be taken soon. A few nobles in Luvic d'Orselle's entourage then decided to intervene with him in favor of the Maid; the time had come to prevail upon the dauphin to make one final military effort. If he didn't, he would never be able to reconquer his kingdom.

At last the captain gave the authorization demanded of him. Liane obtained an escort of six armed men, and they were to be joined by the two astrologers, who said that they wanted to take advantage of this protection to go to the dauphin's court and offer him their services. And thus, on a glacial morning, the little troop started west.

This journey across a region occupied by the enemy was full of risks. Brigands and pillagers of all nationalities controlled the highways; Liane and her companions had to ride by night, taking little-frequented roads and sleeping out in the open fields or in isolated farm houses.

The two astrologers had never experienced anything like this journey, and they found the discomforts hard to bear. Alterdo, however, was in a triumphant mood, for his cyclical theories of history had received an initial confirmation: Noldaz, like the ancient Earth, was to have a heroine who would save her countrymen from the domination of their enemies. If everything happened as Alterdo prophesied, Liane would eventually liberate Irnu and have her king crowned there. Alterdo's favorite axiom would thus be confirmed: "To identical stars, similar planets and comparable histories."

"Perhaps . . ." replied Tiadann. "This young peasant girl is apparently about to become a new Joan of Arc. The kingdom, at war for so many years, needs a hero around whom to rally. A man would have done just as well. Nevertheless, I by no means consider myself beaten. The slightest incident may completely change the mission of our warrior Maid. For example, just authorize me to let some bands of robbers know of her presence in the region. I guarantee that if she were to disappear, the history of Noldaz would make no mention of her . . ."

"My dear friend, you seem to have already forgotten the terms of our agreement: we are absolutely forbidden to make any direct intervention in Lonkian affairs! I admit, however, that your suggestion is a tempting one: as I see it, if Liane of Erck fails to reach the dauphin, another girl will take her place."

"Well, then, give me free rein!"

"That's completely out of the question. When we returned home I would be deprived of my university post for so grave a dereliction. We are here as observers only, don't forget that. Any intervention must be of a very minor nature."

"Oh, all right," grumbled Tiadann. "But orders like that are completely illogical! How can you possibly study a science if you can't experiment?"

"History is very different from the other scientific disciplines, and you know this as well as I do. The Noldazians must be allowed to follow their evolution without interference until such time as their technological progress is sufficient for them to be accepted into the Galactic Confederation."

"Let's not talk about it anymore . . . I only said what I did to shorten what is turning out to be an extremely uncomfortable stay on this primitive planet . . ."

"Patience . . . Our journey will take only about ten days or so, and once we get to the dauphin's court you'll be comfortable enough again!"

Despite Tiadann's ardent wishes, no significant incident disrupted the expedition. Eleven days after her departure the Maid came in sight of Wronais, the dauphin's residence. She stopped for a time in a small chapel to thank the saints who had protected her, then she dictated a letter addressed to Sranz VII. In it the Maid told him that she knew a great deal about him, and she claimed she would recognize him among all the nobles of his court, even though she had never before seen him.

That done, Liane entered the city. The two astrologers happily regained the comfort of an inn: they were beginning to become accustomed to their envelope of flesh and were growing increasingly fond of Lonkian cuisine.

Intrigued by the young girl's letter, the dauphin sent several priests to see her so he could be assured that he was not dealing with some kind of schemer.

Liane did not in the least allow herself to be overawed by these divines: she repeated that she had been sent by the King of Heaven to lift the siege of Fnar and to have the dauphin crowned king in the holy city of Irnu.

The report given the dauphin by the ecclesiastics was so favorable that Liane was summoned to the palace the very next day, accompanied by Alterdo and Tiadann.

"Our gentle Maid will have a great deal of trouble

identifying Sranz among such an assembly," noted the professor as he took in the crowd of courtiers who pressed into the vast hall.

"You needn't worry about her," whispered his colleague. "That girl knows what she's doing. If she has agreed to such a test, it's because she's absolutely sure she can recognize the dauphin."

"We'll soon see! But remember, you're not to intervene!"

Liane, dressed simply in the costume in which she had made the journey, presented a striking contrast to all those nobles in gold-embroidered justicoats and all those fine ladies whose long-trained robes rivaled one another in elegance. There were more than three hundred nobles present.

Taking the Maid by the hand, the court chamberlain led her up to a count bedecked in finery, but the demoiselle, shaking her head, strode directly toward a sad-faced, scowling, somewhat ugly man. Once she stood before him, she made a deep bow and declared, "Gentle Dauphin, may the Lord our God grant you long life . . ."

A murmur of astonishment ran through the crowd. When silence was restored, the dauphin asked Liane:

"Who are you, sweet lady, and what do you want of me?"

"My name is Liane of Erck, and many call me the Maid. I am sent by the King of Heaven to tell you that you must be crowned and anointed in the holy city of Irnu. Then you will be the lieutenant of the King of Heaven, who is also the King of Lonk."

"Those are fine words, my girl! And imposing counsel too, but how am I to be sure that you speak the truth?"

"Gentle Sire, it is not fitting that I give you proofs

of my good faith before all these people. Therefore, prithee grant me private audience . . ."

"Let it be as you wish!"

Sranz led the Maid to a corner of the room and signaled the courtiers to move away. There was then an animated exchange between the young girl and the dauphin. What did she reveal to him? Nobody ever knew. Whatever it was, Sranz seemed greatly interested and quite convinced of Liane's good faith, because after this conversation he gave orders for the newcomer to be lodged in one of the towers of the castle and he assigned a page and a lady-in-waiting to her service.

But things remained unsettled. The dauphin's entourage did not look kindly upon this peasant girl who threatened to replace them. Thinking to gain time, they therefore persuaded Sranz to have the Maid of Fnar interrogated by a commission of theologians. Tongues wagged mightily, and many of the courtiers wondered if this Maid was not in reality a bastard of the Fnar family, since that would explain the reception she had received. To tell the truth, they were completely unable to understand how a simple peasant girl could so quickly have won the friendship of their sovereign.

Alterdo and Tiadann profited from the delay to establish relations among the courtiers so that they could be authorized to follow the Maid on her coming expedition to Fnar which, as they saw it, could not be long put off.

Alterdo kept to his role of astrologer and quickly created a well-merited reputation for himself. As for Tiadann, he seemed to be more drawn to the knights and the men of arms. He bought a suit of armor and a steed and began participating in jousts, in which he gave a very honorable account of himself. Thanks to the gold in their moneybags, they were able to keep open house for all those who visited them in the rooms they had rented near the center of town. Knights and equerries alike appreciated the generosity of these two strangers, who never denied a loan and were always willing to be of service. In addition, the ladies frequently sought out Alterdo for soothsaying or the gift of a love potion. They rarely had any complaint about the efficacy of the drugs, or about the extremely reasonable prices. In short, by the time the theologians gave Liane their wholehearted approval, the two strangers had made a great number of friends.

Events continued to unfold as the professor had foreseen: the heroine had been accepted by the dauphin as a messenger of heaven, and she was going to be in a position to demonstrate her military prowess.

Tiadann was biding his time. He would have loved to modify the course of events by direct intervention, but his honorable colleague kept a close eye on him and constantly emphasized that they were absolutely forbidden by the Confederation to interfere in the affairs of primitive civilizations.

The dauphin had by this time regained confidence in the legitimacy of his claim to the throne: he no longer feared that he might be a bastard, and he was warming to the idea of being crowned king.

Liane was assigned an equerry, guards, and even a chaplain. Sranz set about assembling a vast host, the Maid was newly equipped from head to toe. Her appearance had changed considerably since that visit to Luvic d'Orselle: her long brown hair had been cut so that she could comfortably wear a helmet. (The latter was purposely made without a visor so that everybody could see her face and recognize her.) An iron corselet made to her size closely molded her young form, a short braconniere girdled her waist, and her greave-sheathed legs tightly gripped the flanks of her white palfrey. Strenuous exercise had heightened her color and increased her charm.

Everybody fought for the honor of training her in the use of arms, and she soon became reasonably expert in the art of jousting. Then, when an offer was made to give her a banner belonging to the kings of Lonk, she refused, preferring a standard which, she said, was to be found in a church she had visited upon her arrival. A messenger was dispatched to the church to find the all-white banner bearing a golden dragon over which towered the Archangel Lignel. Nobody had known of its existence, and so all were amazed by this marvel; the prestige of the Maid increased.

To Tiadann's joy, the incident of the banner differed slightly from the ancient Earth legend concerning Joan of Arc in which the chronicles spoke not of a standard but of a magic sword. But Alterdo reminded him that he had never pretended history repeated itself down to the slightest details. As far as he was concerned, it was remarkable how parallel most of the events had been until then.

One sunny though somewhat chilly day in April the host moved out from its assembly point and started toward Fnar, which was still holding out against its besiegers. In her naïveté, Liane expressed the desire to meet with the noble Hechtir, leader of the besieging armies, so that she might simply enjoin him to lift the siege . . . The Lonks refused to allow her to meet with the Incl leader: to do so, it would have been necessary to pass close to the fortresses in which their adversaries were solidly entrenched. That meant running the risk of being cut off in the rear. They therefore took no account of her wishes and crossed the river Mulaz, which bathed the edge of Fnar, at a point well upstream. This enabled them to travel through a fertile region controlled by their own forces, and to approach Fnar from a side that was not blocked by enemy fortifications. In spite of Liane's protests—she would have preferred to attack the besiegers immediately—the maneuver was a success. The Maid's troops and the Lonkian forces within Fnar were joined without a blow having been struck.

The welcome given Liane by the inhabitants was delirious. Everywhere banners bearing the Lonkian colors hung from windows, and a deafening clamor greeted the hardy soldiers whose armor was darkened by the dust of the roads. Hope was reborn: the army brought with it groaning chariots loaded with foodstuffs, the shortage of which was beginning to be sharply felt in the city.

Alterdo was unrestrained in the expression of his triumph. As for Tiadann, he admired the multicolored flags, the artisans' shops, and the churches topped by minarets formed of lovingly carved stones. He felt strangely close to these good people mingling with the new arrivals, and he willingly accepted the embraces of the women who showered their liberators with scarves and flowers.

The men were billeted with the inhabitants. All day long choral canticles rang through the city. Finally, in the evening, as a storm threatened in the lowering sky, the soldiers were allowed to take a well-merited rest. The next day, Liane and her captains took stock of the situation: numerical superiority was with the

Lonks, who had also regained their self-confidence. All they had to do now was raise the siege.

This was no simple matter: though they hadn't completely taken over Fnar, the Incls, experts in the military arts, had established strongly fortified positions. The protective walls circling Fnar bordered the river on the south, and the bridge linking it to the other bank had been cut at the beginning of the siege. Four forts commanded the far end: two on an isle and two others on the river bank. On both the east and the west, the Incls were strongly entrenched.

Liane passionately desired a peaceful resolution of the conflict. Bloodshed and slaughter filled her with horror, and she insisted that the first thing to do was establish contact with the Incls. When her captains came together in council, they decided that such a procedure would merely be a waste of time. Nevertheless, the Maid went to the end of the truncated bridge and, making a megaphone of her hands, summoned the Incls to lift the siege and leave the country. She promised to allow them to depart in peace.

Needless to say, the gruff Incl warriors made mock of her, abusing her thoroughly and calling her a mad, perverted girl. How could an Incl even imagine lowering his colors before a Lonk, and a woman at that? And so each army remained in place, and the Lonkian captains once more met in council.

At this point, bad news arrived: a dust-covered messenger brought word that a relief army was hastening to the aid of the Incls. There was no time to be lost. Liane finally got her captains to go into action, and the Lonks attacked the fort situated east of Fnar.

Despite their numerical superiority, the business began badly for the besieged. The first lines of attackers quickly turned heel and fled. Before they would return to the battle, the Maid had to exhort them and raise their spirits. The presence of this courageous girl at their side doubled the courage of the Lonks, who furiously relaunched the assault and captured the redoubt before the surprised Incls could regroup and counterattack.

It was the first victory the partisans of the dauphin had achieved in years, and it meant that henceforth the city could be freely resupplied. The enthusiasm of the victors was indescribable . . . Once again canticles and martial songs rang through Fnar.

Liane, however, had still not given up hope of finding a peaceful solution to the conflict. She dispatched to the enemy lines a messenger bearing a missive enjoining the Incls to withdraw from Lonk. This time, too, taunts were the only reply. The next day, therefore, after all had rested, hostilities were continued. Crossing the river on a bridge of boats, the Lonks attacked one of the forts on the southern bank. At their head, Liane waved her banner and urged them on.

And then something astonishing happened: the Incls fled in haste without even giving battle! They sought refuge in a better-defended fortification in front of the old bridge but still on the south bank.

Alas! This time the Lonkian captains lacked daring. In spite of the Maid's exhortations, they withdrew their troops. Suddenly the Incls regained confidence and counterattacked; their volleys of arrows soon leaving the Lonks in an awkward position.

It was then that Tiadann, who was enthusiastically fighting in their ranks, made an important discovery. Once again the computers had missed a detail that explained the multiple successes of the invaders. The fact was that at certain crucial moments of battle the Incls made use of projectiles that were tipped with phials containing a volatile liquid, which on impact splashed over the Lonkian armor. This liquid was a toad poison common on the island of the Incls; endowed with powerful incapacitating properties, it caused the Lonks to go into a trance. Soon the very sight of an Incl blazon sent them scurrying!

The crafty historian was careful not to draw his colleague's attention to this diabolical ruse. The fact is, he had some plans of his own and was unwilling to show his hand prematurely.

The Lonks were thus in a sorry situation. But Liane returned to urge them on just as the toxic reaction was beginning to diminish, and she was able to launch a furious counterattack. The battle raged on. Finally, reinforcements from Fnar caused the balance to shift in favor of the Lonks, and the Incls in turn fled wildly and sought refuge behind their ramparts of wood and heaped-up soil. But a breach was soon opened in these when the Lonkian artillery went into action.

The position was quickly taken by assault, and the entire eastern sector of the investment was now in the hands of the Lonks. Astonished by their victory, the dauphin's captains were reluctant to push their luck too far; they therefore quietly awaited reinforcements before continuing the action. Some even wanted to withdraw into Fnar.

But this wasn't the way Liane saw things. She managed to convince the leaders of the troops to set up camp on the site of the victory so that the next day they could continue the attack against the fortification controlling the old bridge: a gate surrounded by four strong stone towers. The attack was launched at dawn on the south side. Since the bridge had been cut, the Incls had no fear of being taken from the rear.

As was his custom, Tiadann accompanied the soldiers, staying close to Liane so that he could keep an eye on what she did and what happened to her.

Suddenly the Maid was struck by an arrow. Tumbling from her horse, she fell to the ground and for a moment remained motionless. Tiadann hastened to her, helped her to her feet, and then lifting her onto her horse, led her from the melee. A hasty inspection showed that her wound presented him with no serious problem. The galactic visitor cut the shaft and freed the arrowhead; then, with the aid of a balm brought from his spaceship, he dressed the wound. Soon the astonished Lonks saw Liane get to her feet, apparently cured.

"Sir," she said to Tiadann, "I owe you many thanks! By heaven there never was a more skillful physician! Henceforth rest assured of my gratitude. Liane never forgets a good turn . . ."

The historian bowed modestly while the Maid put on her armor again before remounting her steed and galloping toward the fort.

The battle went on until evening and still the Lonks were unable to bring it to a successful conclusion. Seeing that their troops were exhausted, the captains wanted to withdraw behind the sheltering walls of Fnar, but Liane managed to get them to agree to a final assault as soon as the soldiers had taken some rest.

Tiadann was worried; the Incls were far from defeated and there was still talk about the arrival of reinforcements. Liane's troops, worn out, showed no desire to go back into the fray.

The Maid was asleep. Tiadann came to a decision, and seizing her banner, profited from the semi-darkness to race toward the ramparts, calling as he went for the Lonks to follow him. They, taking him for the Maid, fell in behind and began attacking once more. Meanwhile, from the side closest to Fnar, some knights had set a gangway over the standing arch of the destroyed bridge and surprised the Incls from the rear. Liane, awakened by the tumult and embarrassed at having allowed herself to drop off to sleep, returned to the front ranks and retrieved her banner. Troubled, she wondered if this valiant stranger, whose eyes shone so brightly when they rested on her, was not indeed some archangel sent by Lignel . . .

The young girl's courage and faith were strengthened by this idea: henceforth, nothing could withstand the furor of the Lonks. Their adversaries, refusing to surrender, were cut down to the very last man. Some jumped into the river, where, pulled down by the weight of their armor, they drowned; others were put to the sword.

The Maid had accomplished her first task: the next morning, when the Lonks approached the last enemy strongholds, they saw the accursed Incls fleeing as fast as their legs could carry them. Liane gave orders to allow them to depart.

In the liberated city of Fnar the reveling Lonks shouted their joy while the priests intoned canticles of thanksgiving, and the bells rang out in triumphant peals.

Tiadann rejoined his friend Alterdo, who had remained behind during these memorable days, safely sampling a few bottles of good wine.

"Well, what do you say now?" asked the professor. "Apparently things went just as I said they would!"

"I have to admit that you've been right up to now . . . The Maid has kept the first part of her promise. It remains to be seen if she will as easily manage to have her dauphin crowned and then chase the Incls from his kingdom."

"No problem! It's all been recorded in advance in the Great Book of History, my dear Tiadann. 'To identical stars. . . .' "

"I know, I know!" grumbled his assistant. "Instead of babbling away, you might be better occupied in pouring me something to drink. I'm dying of thirst . . ."

Chapter Two

For several days the host rested; wounds were dressed and booty distributed.

Two notables of the army, the Bastard of Moruns and the Prince of Ardez, had noticed Tiadann's bravery, and when the Maid suggested that he be knighted, they happily agreed to sponsor him. Both knew that he had saved the young girl's life, and at this point Liane's prestige was such that her death would have irreparably compromised their cause.

The two men were extremely different: Moruns, heavyset and dumpy, had a bull-like neck surmounted by a head whose features seemed to have been hacked out with an axe. Blue eyes softened the roughness of his physiognomy. Robust and athletic—there were those who claimed that his strength was inexhaustible—he had broken many a steed under him in the course of his mad rides. His gestures and language had a military bluntness, and his tone of voice was that of a leader accustomed to being obeyed.

As for Ardez, he had all the elegance of a man at home in royal palaces. Slender and agile, he was a past master in the art of swordsmanship. His chin sported a short and well-combed beard, and his penetrating black eyes had a crafty expression that betrayed a cunning man who knew the ins and outs of court trickery. He was always dressed to the hilt and showed a fondness for the rings and gold chains of the numerous knightly orders to which he belonged.

In short, the two men complemented one another marvelously, and though each was slightly jealous of the other, they demonstrated a mutual respect.

The ceremony took place on the battlefield. Ten equerries and some twenty young nobles were admitted to the envied title. All kneeled before their sponsors, who, with the flat of a sword, struck them on the shoulder and spoke the ritual words:

"I dub thee knight! Be valorous, valiant, and humble."

Golden spurs were then set on their feet and they were each given a shield painted with a coat of arms.

Tiadann's blazon was azur and sinople and bore an arrow as a reminder of his great deed.

The Prince of Ardez, after bestowing the accolade upon Tiadann, presented him with a bound volume in which the rules of the order were recorded, whereas Moruns made him a present of a superb sword captured from the Incls. Pennants and banners flapped in the wind and the sun glistened on the armor of the noble retinue.

Alterdo, who witnessed this ceremony, could not help but admire his friend's sober grandeur. Nevertheless, he was troubled: the fact was that Tiadann's fame could result in his being given a high post in the army, and this did not at all accord with the normal course of history. However, Alterdo kept telling himself that there was no reason not to fraternize with the aborigines as long as no attempt was made to modify the unfolding of events.

Ten days after the victory, the army left the city of Fnar. Weeping tears of joy, all the inhabitants, burghers and serfs, accompanied the young girl who had liberated them.

The host moved toward the southwest to join up with the dauphin, and the two armies met before the city of Ourmoy. This time, Sranz threw his arms effusively around the Maid in a gesture of gratitude, and then they all went off to their quarters in the city.

Liane had hoped to continue her military operations without delay, but she was to be disappointed; in the long discussions that followed, Moruns, Ardez, and the other captains found themselves in disagreement. Many Lonks could not quite accept the fact that they had beaten the Incls so easily, and they now feared a new encounter; some even went so far as to urge that the army be disbanded. Others supported the Maid and emphasized that the leader of the enemy forces, Rog Bacdir, was reassembling troops in order to wipe out the defeat inflicted on his compatriots.

As for Tiadann, he adopted a wait-and-see attitude in order not to arouse Alterdo's suspicions. He often met with Liane, who held him in high esteem and appreciated his counsel. And thus it was that under the pledge of secrecy the cunning fellow was told a detail that threw more light on the recent victories. Though he had already discovered the secret for himself during the siege of Fnar, he now had to swear not to disclose it–something he was willing enough to do, since he was in no way eager to take his friend Alterdo into his confidence.

The fact of the matter was, the Maid explained, that the deadly arrows of the Incl crossbows had incapacitating properties . . . Until now this mysterious substance had permitted the invaders to achieve great victories when they launched a hail of arrows at crucial moments of the battles.

As it happened, the crafty Liane, daughter of the fields, knew the virtues of simples. Talkative peddlers had told her of the magical effects of the toad poison used by the Incls and had confided the secret of the antidote in exchange for a few coins: it was sufficient to chew on the leaves of a climbing blackberry vine for the effects of the poison to be counteracted. Happily, vines of this type were extremely common in the kingdom of Lonk.

During her solitary walks at dawn, the Maid had gathered an ample store of these leaves, and she had distributed them to her soldiers before the battle, thereby counteracting the effects of the Incl secret weapon!

This explained her victories: the Lonk soldiers were every bit as good as their adversaries—when they fought on equal terms.

Tiadann vowed to exploit this method to his advantage—he was an expert in chemical and biological weapons. With his aid, Liane could accomplish great things, but he was careful not to disclose his skills, merely awaiting his hour. . . .

After interminable palavers, the dauphin appointed the Prince of Ardez leader of the army; Moruns was made his second in command. Operations started up again immediately. The problem now was to open the road to the holy city: Irnu. One after another the occupied towns between it and Fnar were liberated. In addition, one of the most famous Incl captains was taken prisoner.

Suddenly, the invaders began sueing for a truce. It was the first time in years that they had been willing to negotiate, but Liane refused. Flying from victory to victory, her army came up against two enemy corps, one commanded by Hechtir and the other by

Rog Bacdir. In spite of their number and their bravery, the Incls were thoroughly defeated and Hechtir taken prisoner.

Henceforth, there was no possible doubt: the Maid had been sent by the King of Heaven. She even foretold the future, warning the knights of the manner in which they would die. Her renown spread throughout the country and songs celebrating her prowess were composed.

> *In one four hundred twenty-nine*
> *The sun began to shine*
> *It brought back the good old days*
> *The almost forgotten ways*

And there was something to sing about: before the arrival of Liane, two thousand Lonks could be defeated by one thousand Incls. Now the invaders were fleeing before their adversaries!

Tiadann had played some small part in the last victory: he had revealed the presence of Incl archers in a forest into which the Lonkian knights were unguardedly riding.

To do this, he had taken over the spirit of a noble woodland animal and sent the latter running right toward the Incl archers, who had been unable to keep themselves from shooting at the magnificent beast and thereby revealing their presence.

Nobody saw anything strange in the incident, not even Alterdo, though the scholar was extremely suspicious of his colleague. Each time they met, he would say the same thing:

"What's the good of being so stubborn, Tiadann? You can see for yourself that everything is happening just as the history computers said it would. Fnar is free, and now that the Incls have suffered a great defeat the dauphin will be crowned at Irnu. Soon the Lonks will chase their enemies from the kingdom. I think it's time to leave this planet."

"Not at all, my friend! I agree that you have foreseen the situation correctly: this heroine is faithfully following the path of her historical counterpart. Nevertheless, none of this is proof that her great good luck will continue. A mere nothing would suffice to upset the apple cart. For example, on several occasions the Lonks have refused to follow her orders. In addition, the Incls still occupy a large part of the country, and their allies in the south have yet to be heard from. . . . There's no hurry. Don't you enjoy studying this medieval civilization up close?"

"Yes, of course . . . But I think that I have enough information about them at this point. In any case, this lifestyle is so different from ours—no computers, no robots—that I feel rather lost."

"We applied for an absence of fifty local years, and I see no reason to leave now."

"My dear Tiadann, I don't want to offend you, since you have always demonstrated such a passionate interest in our art. Indeed, that's why I chose you as my assistant. But this time I think you are too involved in our experiment: I know that history has to be judged on the evidence and that eyewitnesses and authenticated reports are better than secondary sources. But you have managed to become a person of importance here. The Maid herself sees you often and seems to take pleasure in your company. Be careful not to exceed our rights here and meddle in the affairs of this society. Given your skills, the temptation is a great one. Keep in mind that such behavior can lead nowhere. As soon as we return, everything we have done will be closely analyzed, and any modification we may have made in the history of this country will be rectified. I suppose I needn't mention the sanctions that would be imposed. . . ."

"You're not telling me anything I don't know," interrupted Tiadann. "I've done nothing reprehensible. As a knight, I am able to mingle with the great of this world and learn more about it in a month than our spy satellites can in ten years!"

"That's perfectly correct, and it's the reason I've made no attempt to keep you from doing things your way. I was merely giving you a warning, my friend, And I hope you won't take what I've said amiss. Since you want to continue our experiment, let's stay. . . . However, we won't learn anything of importance from now on. Like all heroines, this Liane has aroused jealousy and dissatisfaction. The dauphin's councillors are unhappy about her growing influence, and she's sure to come to a bad end. I'm afraid you will be upset by that, since you seem to have become very attached to this young girl."

"Don't worry about me!" Tiadann interrupted. "There may be some surprises in store for you: that Maid has formed vast projects, and she may still astonish you."

"Let's hope you're right," concluded Alterdo, yawning. "I'm beginning to find this experiment boring. . . ."

The march against Irnu continued methodically as one after another the enemy strongholds fell. Tiadann always took part in the battles, while his friend remained at the dauphin's court, amusing himself and leading the good life. He was still very popular with the ladies and was about to become appointed astrologer to Sranz himself.

The campaign for the liberation of Irnu was very different from the previous battles. The host moved with its artillery and its heavy wagons, its size increasing as former dissidents joined the ranks. Among the turncoats were some notables whom the Maid unhesitatingly welcomed, and this provoked jealousy among those military leaders who had remained loyal all along. Tiadann made a discreet contribution to the army's success by generalizing the use of wheels to transport the bombards and culverins. He also standardized the caliber of the various weapons and insisted that all ammunition be of uniform dimensions, a factor which increased the accuracy of Lonkian fire.

The inhabitants of the besieged cities now preferred to negotiate with the Lonks rather than undergo further siege, and thus many of them surrendered without a fight. Oyes itself, the city in which the shameful treaty that delivered the kingdom to the Incls had been signed, was taken only two days after the army arrived before its gates. The garrisons were allowed to flee without being pursued. And thus it was that the army entered Irnu in the month of July. All in all, the expedition had progressed with a somewhat unnerving facility . . .

The dauphin entered the holy city in the company of Liane and the principal Lonkian seigneurs, all decked out in their best finery; heralds carrying his coat of arms preceded the cortege, and trumpets filled the air with their thundering blasts. The spectacle was so imposing that many of the nobles who had sworn loyalty to the Incls now rallied to Sranz. Finally, the coronation ceremony took place in the marvelous cathedral of Irnu.

Tiadann was dazzled by so much magnificence and didn't know where to look first. He was fascinated by the glowing stained glass, by the delicate stone tracery of the capitals, and by the finery of the ladies with their headdresses and laces.

The timid dauphin received the crown and was anointed by the high priest. As a celestial music resounded, choirs of angelic purity joined with the deep sound of the silver organs. The nave of the church was completely bathed by the aromatic incense burning in hundreds of vermeil pots.

And so while Liane brandished her banner high, the dauphin became Sranz VII, absolute and legitimate sovereign of the Lonks. The Maid could not keep from weeping tears of joy. . . . Afterward the cortege moved through the main streets of the city while the crowd roared: "Long live the King of Lonk. Blessed be our sovereign!"

The suffocating heat of that beautiful summer month played its part in the success of the celebrations that followed: more than one burgher of that good city stayed outdoors all night and ended up as drunk as a lord! As for the Chevalier Tiadann, he participated in the banquet together with Liane's faithful followers. The enormous table groaned under the victuals. The king occupied the place of honor, and Liane was on his right.

The Bastard of Moruns, whose influence in the army grew with each passing day, found himself sitting opposite Tiadann, on whose left sat the Prince of Ardez, one of the fiercest partisans of the heroine of the day. On Tiadann's right was Liane's equerry, a robust and blunt-spoken fellow who always jealously watched over the Maid—even tasting everything put on her plate—and who spent his nights sleeping before the door to her chamber. He was in a surly humor because it seemed to him that on this day of revels and madness his protegé was not being carefully enough guarded.

"Zounds!" he swore, "these prettified lords seem better suited to telling silly stories than to striking hearty blows. I would stake my life on it that all these ladies' men haven't seen an Incl banner for years. . . . They're swarming around Liane like flies around a honey pot! And just look at this table—there's enough here to feed an entire company! What waste! The whole court's rotten to the core! If I were the Maid, I'd send them all packing!"

"You're right, my good friend!" agreed Tiadann with conviction. "Without Liane all these beautiful people would be dying of hunger in some tumble-down castle. Ah! believe me, the Maid still has some surprises in store for us!"

"That's right, chevalier," interjected the Bastard of Moruns. "And I would like you to settle an argument between Ardez and myself. He claims that it would be dangerous to advance on Aniar, our capital. The prince fears that the troops of the Duke of Xovia, allied with the Incls . . ."

"Precisely!" interrupted the prince. "Our southern frontier is badly manned, and there's nothing to prevent the Xovians from attacking us in the rear. In addition, the Incl troops are still numerous; don't forget that the garrisons of the liberated cities were allowed to withdraw freely! Moruns is too bold."

Tiadann had his own ideas about this, as his computers had provided him with information that Liane's partisans did not have.

"The problem is a difficult one," he said in a worried tone. "The Xovians cannot be ignored. However, I've heard it said that certain of our king's councillors have secretly been negotiating with the Duke of

Xovia for the restitution of our capital. The Maid herself is in favor of a reconciliation. Didn't she urge the duke to come to the coronation of Sranz VII? It's claimed that his ambassadors have just arrived and that they propose, if granted a fifteen-day truce, to surrender Aniar, where they command the garrison. I am convinced that the negotiations with the Xovians will be fruitful."

"'Sdeath!" swore the bastard, "can't you see that they're only playing for time? The Incls are stirring up their men to defend Aniar, and I have learned from a reliable source that an army is crossing the channel to reinforce the occupation troops! We've got to strike against these dogs without delay. . . ."

"I share Moruns' opinion," added the Prince of Ardez, shifting his previous point of view. "The thing to do is strike while the iron is hot. I will use all my influence to see to it that the army starts off for Aniar as soon as possible!"

"That's my advice, too, noble friends," agreed Tiadann. "There is absolutely no doubt that we will soon liberate the capital. Afterward, if the Xovians can be counted on to respect a truce, we can easily boot the Incls out of the kingdom of Lonk. But I might go even further: do you really think we should be satisfied with that? The Duke of Fnar is still a prisoner on the island of the Incls. Why shouldn't we cross the channel and free him?"

"Now that's the way to talk!" thundered the Bastard of Moruns. "For decades those barefaced thieves have been laying our country waste. I'd like a chance to do the same to theirs!

"A seaborne invasion? If we're to do that, we'll have to have control of the coastal cities . . ." objected the prince, lowering his voice.

"That needn't be a problem!" rumbled Tiadann. "Once our capital has been liberated, why not strike right toward the sea? You may have noticed that our army gains reinforcements as it moves along. All the nobles are rallying to it! If a thousand of us set off, we'll be ten thousand by the time we arrive . . ."

"What you suggest is a vast undertaking," remarked the Prince of Ardez solemnly. "I admit the idea intrigues me greatly, but I would wager that the king's advisers will not take kindly to the notion. They're always counseling delay and are still afraid to hazard too much. . . ."

"Well, time will show!" exclaimed the brave bastard. "For my part, I agree with our friend Tiadann: we have to go after the beast in his own lair. . . ."

The discussion ceased as the king left the hall.

In the weeks that followed, the royal army quit Irnu and headed south. As it went along, it liberated innumerable strongholds, and many soldiers joined its ranks. Nevertheless, Sranz VII still hesitated. When the host arrived at the banks of the Rifen, which traversed the capital upstream, far from where they were, he renounced the idea of crossing it and headed back north.

The Incl regent, Rog Bacdir, then sent him a message in which he contested his title of king. As was his custom, the rog freely insulted the Maid, treating her as "a loose and dissolute woman who dared to wear men's clothes." Then he defied Sranz to come against his army and advised him to surrender. For once the milksop Sranz was stung to the quick, and one month after his coronation, the two armies were face to face. Liane, Moruns, and Tiadann exulted: a decisive encounter was finally going to take place! Alas! After a few skirmishes the Incls withdrew and Sranz took advantage of the situation to regain the comfort of Wronais castle.

The Lonkian army listlessly followed the enemy, freeing as it passed several cities near the capital. Then the negotiations with the Duke of Xovia, still watchful on the southern borders of the kingdom, took a favorable turn. The truce was to last until the end of the year! It was a catastrophe for Liane and her partisans, because this truce spread throughout the country. . . . Thanks to a strange clause, however, Aniar was excluded from the truce, so the Xovians could even fight alongside the Incls if the capital were attacked!

Furious, the Prince of Ardez had a bridge of boats thrown across the Rifen in order to begin preparations for taking the city. The king remained evasive. Deciding that the only way to deal with this pusillanimous and easily influenced monarch was to adopt a strong hand, Ardez went to fetch him and bring him back to the bosom of the army. The precious time lost had allowed the Incls and their Xovian allies to build up their forces, but at last the attack got underway.

Unfortunately, the Lonks had a run of bad luck: Liane was badly wounded during the battle. Only Tiadann's intelligent care made a quick recovery possible. But something even more serious happened. An Incl arrow struck the page who was brandishing the Maid's banner, and the symbol of reconquered liberty fell to the dust. From that time on, many Lonks were convinced that the Maid had lost her magic powers. . . .

The king gave orders to retreat. It was Liane's first defeat.

Alterdo saw nothing unusual in these events. It was the beginning of the ineluctable decline of the heroine, who according to the pitiless laws of history, was soon to die, rejected by her countrymen.

Tiadann, however, did not see things in the same way. Determined to modify the history of this planet as he saw fit, he had until now been restrained by a few lingering scruples. After this disaster, he decided to go into action.

Matters came to a head when Alterdo, learning that Tiadann had treated Liane with remedies that came from their spaceship, reproached him bitterly.

"This time you're going too far!" he declared. "Not content with taking part in the battles and urging the Maid's partisans to fight to the death, you make use of our remedies to cure her. Once we return, you'll have to answer for what you've done, and I guarantee that I won't go easy on you! What about those promises you made?"

"They don't mean a thing to me! How can you be so narrow-minded? Here we have a marvelous field for experimentation on this planet, and you want to keep me from intervening? How little you know me!"

"What do you mean by that?"

"My illustrious imbecile friend, you are undoubtedly about to be astonished by what I have to say: if you intended to leave this planet, don't count on our spaceship. I've secretly stolen the control key you need to bring the ship down, and it's therefore impossible for you to send out a distress signal. There's nothing you can do, and you're completely in my power. It's my intention to modify the history of this planet as I see fit, and there's no way you can stop me!"

"What's this? You must be completely out of your mind!" exclaimed Alterdo as he rummaged through his baggage and discovered that his friend had told the truth. "I beg of you, think it over while there's still time! Celsar, don't try this experiment! Even if you succeed in changing the course of events, our compatriots will find out about it and a temporal patrol will come to straighten things out! You will be punished as an example to others, with at least a hundred years of imprisonment on an asteroid. Listen, if you return my signal key and leave Noldaz with me immediately, I promise not to say anything about this. . . . You'll have nothing to fear. I give you my word!"

"Humbug! I've excellent reasons for not worrying about the Confederation: when we left, I falsified our mission orders. Nobody knows where we are. So far as I'm concerned, the patrol can start searching for us among the millions of planets! That ought to give me time enough to amuse myself down here. . . ."

"You can't seriously be considering ending your life among these aborigines?"

"To tell the truth, I find the idea quite attractive! At home I was just an ordinary assistant with no power at all. Here, I'm on the way to becoming somebody of importance."

"Celsar, you're raving! I beg you once again . . ."

"Bah! You and your nonsense are beginning to bore me. From now on, I'm in command. And just to prove it to you, I'm going to have you thrown into one of their dungeon cells."

"Under what pretext?" asked Alterdo, stiffening.

"Heresy, my friend! You made a mistake when you disguised yourself as an astrologer. People of that sort are looked upon with suspicion in this country, especially if they happen not to be charlatans. You were too eager to shine in the eyes of the ladies—your predictions were too accurate. Now you'll have to answer to an ecclesiastical court for your behavior."

"Traitor and liar! . . . Celsar, profit from your triumph while you can. The Tarpeian Rock is not far from the Capitol . . ."

"Save your classical citations for somebody who can appreciate them!" snickered the chevalier. "Guards! Take the prisoner away . . ."

Two equerries came to seize the poor wretch; overwhelmed by this stroke of fate, he offered absolutely no resistance.

And then Tiadann went into action.

Sole possessor of all the instruments carried aboard the spaceship, he spent some time in a distant wood where the ship had landed on his orders. There he synthesized a quick-acting drug endowed with incapacitating properties allied to neuroleptic action. Its absorption after aerosol dispersion made any human easily influenceable during a brief period of time. It was in this way that he planned to get Sranz VII to make important decisions that would place the king entirely in his power. . . .

Several days later, after his spaceship had regained the synchronous orbit which allowed it to spy permanently on the kingdom of Lonk, the crafty Tiadann was received in audience by the king. The Bastard of Moruns and the Prince of Ardez were with him, although neither of them had been taken into his confidence.

The monarch had already given orders to make preparations for his departure from the combat zone. He was eager to return to his beloved Wronais Castle, where he could once more take up his peaceful pursuits in the company of his court.

Looking peevish, the king was seated near the fireplace. He was teasing some grayhounds with a branch, and they were barking furiously. Not far off, stood his usual dining companions and his favorite councillors.

"Please be brief, gentlemen," he said sullenly as he turned from the dogs. "We can only grant you a moment. . . ."

Without further ado, Tiadann knelt before him and activated his aerosol micro-disperser.

"Sire," he said, "I would be loath to intrude upon Your Majesty if the interest of the kingdom did not make it necessary for me to request this audience. . . ."

The drug was already taking effect: Sranz's eyes became vague and he was smiling.

"Speak. You know We are always open to suggestions that come from such worthy chevaliers as yourself."

"Evil councillors have led you to make unfortunate decisions, Sire. Your capital city awaits your pleasure. . . ."

"What do you mean by that?"

"Simply that if you launch a decisive attack, Aniar will fall into your hands like a ripe fruit . . ."

"Upon my soul, you seem very sure of what you are saying. All my councillors have told me just the opposite. Our assault has been thrown back. The Incls and the Xovians are strongly entrenched, yet you claim that we can dislodge them?"

"Ask Monseigneur of Moruns and the Prince of Ardez, Your Majesty. They will confirm what I say."

"Is this true, gentlemen?"

"By God, Tiadann speaks the truth!" exclaimed the bastard passionately. "These dogs have already been drubbed more than once, and I am convinced that I can make them ignominiously flee our capital."

"I am of the same opinion!" assured the prince. "Our troops are spirited, and they only await your order to attack once more. The Incls and the Xovians must be booted out of Aniar before they receive reinforcements. With the aid of the Maid, we'll gobble them up."

"Gadzooks! You speak the truth, my friends! Ever since Liane came to give us courage, the Incls have been beaten hollow! We have been the plaything of milksops completely lacking in courage, but by the King of Heaven, things are going to change. . . ."

"That's the way to talk, Sire!" Tiadann approved hotly. "Get rid of this rabble that only seeks to enjoy itself at your expense! Replace them by your true friends, those who have fought for Your Majesty since His coronation."

Uneasy at this turn of events, the monarch's familiars had drawn near. Suddenly they saw him leap up and shout:

"By Heaven, you speak the truth! We have too long been deceived by these traitors. The Archangel Lignel has given Liane a mission, and it is Our duty to give her the means to accomplish it. From this day henceforth Moruns and Liane will command the army as marshals. All my former councillors are to return to their estates and not leave them without orders from me. Ardez will be Our lieutenant general. You, valiant Tiadann, We name you Seneschal of Lonk. Make all dispositions necessary to allow Our host to lay siege to Aniar immediately!"

This sudden change in the king, who was generally inclined to evasiveness, astonished his intimates.

But this time he seemed absolutely determined to be

energetic. The first to rejoice at this was Liane, who warmly thanked Tiadann for his support.

While Moruns recalled those contingents that had already started south, Tiadann set about reorganizing the artillery.

He had already established the use of gun-carriages that made it easy to displace the bombards. Now he modified them with rack and pinion systems for vertical aiming. Then he improved the watertightness of breech-loading cannon by arranging a system of springs and copper joints. For the harquebus, operated by two men, he improved the firing system by devising a touchhole which had a matchlock carried by a lever, which set the lighted wick on the fire-pan. In this way the disastrous effects of rain were modified: the artillery could fire in all weathers. All this of course required time, and not all these modifications were ready for the day of the assault against the capital.

Actually, Tiadann was getting ready for future campaigns. He started the manufacture of handheld culverins worked by two men, and even of a harquebus that could be operated by a single soldier. He also turned his attention to the standardized production of powder, giving orders that each component was to be carefully weighed out and that the powder barrels were to be tarred in order to prevent humidity from seeping in. And thus it was that the traditional weapons—mangonels, trebuchets, and tower-borne crossbows—which made so many Incl successes possible, became outdated.

During this time, the Bastard of Moruns was preparing for the investment of Aniar. A new bridge was built so that a simultaneous attack could be made from both sides of the river.

The signal for the attack was given: flaming barrels of pitch were piled before the wooden palisades that formed the first line of defense. Everything blazed gaily. Then the Lonks found themselves confronting moats filled with water. Lightweight throwbridges had been provided, and overcoming this second obstacle without difficulty, the Lonks obtained the stone ramparts. Liane was in the first ranks of the attackers; her equerry brandished her banner while Tiadann and Moruns protected her as well as they could from the swarms of arrows around her.

And now the artillery had its turn. Drawn by teams of powerful oxen, the bombards were set up within firing range. Thanks to the rack and pinion systems, the weapons could be carefully aimed at the battlements and the wooden doors, and the firing began.

Never in the memory of the Lonks had such precision been seen. The heavy iron cannonballs that rumbled toward the soldiers on the ramparts created veritable carnage. Blood streamed down the crumbling walls. The doors did not hold out for long and were soon dismantled. With Liane at their head, the Lonks rushed through the gaping breach.

Inside the city, the Xovians and the Incls stiffened their resistance, but Tiadann had his first tripod harquebuses brought up. The men who operated them placed the end of the cannon on a forked prop, and the front ranks of the Lonks drew back: the projectiles fired point-blank into the mass of defenders and sowed panic among them.

A few hours after the assault began, Aniar was in the hands of Sranz VII, who was unable to get over this unexpected success.

Accounts were already being settled. Overzealous collaborators were imprisoned and Aniar partisans of

Sranz came to swell the ranks of his army. The Incl leader and a Xovian count were captured. This time few of the enemy escaped, since the city had been attacked from two sides simultaneously.

The bells were pealing thunderously when the king, with Liane on his left, made his entrance into the principal church. Behind them—their armor still blackened and bloodied—Tiadann, Moruns, and Ardez, watched the spectacle with broad smiles.

Tiadann seemed particularly happy: this first serious deviation from the historical development of the planet had been accomplished without great difficulty. The future belonged to him. Soon the Incls would be chased from the kingdom of Lonk: then there would be time to think of more serious things. . . .

Chapter Three

Henceforth, Sranz VII was nothing but a puppet whose strings were pulled by Tiadann. He attended the sessions of the Council, but he merely confirmed the decisions already taken by his marshal, his lieutenant general, and his seneschal.

The first of these meetings took place in the royal palace of the capital, Aniar. It had been years since a king of Lonk had resided there.

Determined to carry his experiment to its conclusion, Tiadann unveiled his intentions craftily, screening himself behind Liane, whom he skillfully manipulated. The Maid, convinced of the sacred nature of her mission, was willing enough to be persuaded of the necessity of carrying out the military campaign unhesitatingly.

"I would wager that the Archangel Lignel is well satisfied!" Tiadann exclaimed. "Our king has been crowned, his capital is liberated, and the Incls will soon be booted out of the kingdom. But we mustn't stop there. Haven't your celestial voices told you to free the Duke of Fnar, who has been languishing in Incl prisons for years now?"

"Upon my soul, Tiadann, you say the truth. You must know better than anyone that God holds the king and the Duke of Fnar equally dear. Heaven's messenger, the Archangel Lignel, often speaks to me while I say my evening prayers in church, and he has commanded me to do everything in my power to free the gentle duke. . . . I have already enjoined Rog Bacdir to send him back to us."

"And how has he replied?"

"With jests and insults, as usual . . ."

"Then our duty seems clear: since the Incls refuse to listen to you, as is their wont, we must needs pursue them to their very island in order to free our loyal duke!"

"In God's name, that is just what I plan to do," roared Moruns. "Those dogs will give us no peace until we have forced them to their knees!"

"Do not invoke the name of the Lord in vain, sweet friend. It breaks my heart to hear you swear so," Liane objected in a gentle voice. "Think of the salvation of your soul!"

"My angel, I confess to this bad habit. For your sake, I will try to control myself. . . ."

"For this, many thanks. . . . You must know that Heaven has imposed on me a task displeasing to a poor girl such as myself. I hate violence, and I cannot bear to see the Hell suffered by the poor wretches wounded in battle. Nevertheless, I am a war leader, and I must continue the fight unceasingly. We will therefore strike against the enemy in the very heart of his refuge. I will, however, once more send word to King Dronz. Mayhap he will agree to free the noble duke. If he does, many lives will be spared."

"A praiseworthy sentiment and one I wholeheartedly endorse," exclaimed Tiadann. "Let us send a messenger to the island of the Incls. But since I fear the king may not deign to reply, we must even now establish a plan of operations so that we are not delayed later."

"That's exactly what I think," agreed the Prince of Ardez. "We must not linger in Aniar. Let us rather follow the Rifen to the sea and free Ronande. This done, our army will have access to the ports we need if we mean to attempt a seaborne invasion."

"Don't you think that may be too vast an undertaking?" the king objected timidly.

"Great balls of fire," stormed Moruns. "I hope Your Majesty will forgive my speaking so freely, but aren't we capable of doing in the present what a Duke of Ronande was able to do in the past? We need only assemble a powerful fleet!"

"We will need time to build one, my good marshal," noted Sranz VII. "The Incls are expert navigators, whereas we have been cut off from the sea for decades. . . ."

"Don't let that worry you, Sire!" said Tiadann. "I know quite a bit about these things, and I am convinced that I can build you ships that will outclass those of the Incls. There are trees enough in your kingdom to provide all the timber we need."

"You are obviously a man of many talents, my dear seneschal. If things are as you say, I can see no further objections."

"Besides, Our army will not be idle during this time," continued the Prince of Ardez. "I have heard tell that Our cousin Xovia is unhappy about Our recent victories. . . ."

"Let's propose a truce to him," suggested Liane.

"That's a judicious idea," said Sranz. "My cousin has just married a rich princess from the south. He will not be eager to disturb his honeymoon by warring against us. In addition, Xovia has recently created a new order of knighthood, and sumptuous feasts are even now being held in his duchy. I wager that he will agree to a brief period of inactivity. I shall immediately dispatch a herald to propose that we each accept a month-long truce."

"Perfect!" exclaimed Tiadann. "In that way we'll have our hands free to deal with Ronande. We must reach the sea before the duke is ready for action again. Sire, give orders for the army to follow the Rifen to its mouth. Let ships be prepared to bring food and supplies along the river."

"Very well, I will give you a signed blank parchment which you can fill in at your leisure, my good seneschal! But what do you propose to do?"

"I thought we might have Monseigneur de Moruns and the Prince of Ardez follow along the south bank, while the Maid and I attack along the north. The ships will enable us to join forces if need be."

"What do you say to this, gentlemen?" the king inquired.

"I share Tiadann's opinion," said the lieutenant-general immediately. "We'll place the fortresses and cities along the Rifen under siege. If we control the two banks of the river, they will be isolated."

"I'm in complete agreement," said Moruns in turn. "Rog Bacdir is retreating along the north bank, but there are still many Incls on the south bank, in Ronande. They must be simultaneously eliminated."

"All-powerful God," said the Maid, clasping her hands in prayer, "let our armies be victorious! But there will be more slaughter. . . . May You lead Bacdir to see the light. May he agree to quit the kingdom of Lonk, may he free the Duke of Fnar—and by the Archangel Lignel I promise to allow him to return to his island in perfect safety! Sire, will you allow me to send him a message exhorting him to listen to reason?"

"You are good and pious, Liane. Do as you wish—but I wager that these mad dogs will not agree to quit Our kingdom without new fighting. Like you, I am saddened by the thought. Alas, I fear we will have to drub them fiercely and let the blood flow before they can be brought to see reason. . . ."

Upon these words from the sovereign, the council ended, and its members immediately went off to inform their captains of what had been decided. Everybody greeted the news enthusiastically, and a week later the host left Aniar and started west.

The first cities fell without a fight; the Incls had withdrawn to fortifications commanding the river, and there they resolutely awaited the Lonks.

Soon, messengers arrived bearing important news. To begin with, insults were the only response to Liane's missive to Bacdir. Abusing her as was his wont, the rog called her a perverted woman and a limb of Satan. More importantly, he declared that his sovereign, Dronz VI, had in his turn just been crowned king of the Lonks and that as a consequence all those fighting under the pseudo-king—Sranz—would be declared traitors to the crown and dealt with as such. Liane's attempt to bring peace had failed: it was obvious that the Incls would fight to the end and accept no compromise.

On the other hand, Sranz's envoys had been well received by the Duke of Xovia, who, eager to gain time, accepted an immediate truce. Thus the Lonks were assured of not being attacked from the rear during their military operations in Ronande—that is, if they acted quickly.

Unfortunately, the heavy ships that followed the

host along the river were soon stopped by a barrier of chains that blocked the Rifen at a point dominated by a powerful fortress: Valiant Castle. This stronghold had been built long ago by one of King Dronz's ancestors in order to control access from the west to the Duchy of Ronande, his fief. The chateau rose on a rocky spur at a point where the Rifen flowed between two sharp cliffs. At its base was an island controlling the river. Whatever the cost, this island had to be taken so that the army could continue on its way. Because the Lonks were overawed by the imposing mass of Valiant Castle, Tiadann took charge of the operations.

Renouard, Liane's equerry, forcefully summed up the situation as follows:

"Hell's bells! These accursed sons of the devil have holed up in a well-fortified lair! Their damned bastille commands the route. I wonder if we'll ever be able to blast them out. . . ."

"That's true enough," agreed his crony, a hardy fellow. "I'd give all my share of the booty if the Archangel Lignel would lend me wings so that I could fly up to the ramparts. Our harquebuses will never hit the target!"

"Bah! We have to have confidence in the Maid, my friend. She's sure to find some way to smoke those dogs out of their castle. I can remember that when we got to Fnar nobody believed Liane would be able to achieve what so many brave captains had failed to do. Well, it didn't take her long: ten days later the Incls were running like scared rabbits!"

In spite of these optimistic words, Valiant Castle seemed impregnable. The double row of river chains kept the ships from sailing past, and the armies along the banks could not proceed without supplies. In addition, the fortress walls were so thick that only the biggest bombards could make a dent in them, and then only if they had been hauled to the top of neighboring heights. This required a superhuman effort, as the weapons were on the ships blocked upstream. . . .

The meeting of the captains directing the assault was therefore a mournful affair: the rog's forces were massing for a counterattack, and if the stronghold wasn't taken quickly, the route to Ronande would be cut.

Tiadann set about raising morale, first by releasing a euphorific aerosol, and then by proposing a simple and bold plan.

"What's the good in persisting!" he declared energetically. "The fortress will fall easily enough if Bacdir can't supply it. Never mind Valiant Castle—let's continue our offensive! We have to meet with the Incl army and defeat it. Once that's done, our hands will be free."

"You can't just dismiss the blasted fort—it commands the river," sighed the Prince of Ardez. "How can we go forward if our ships can't follow behind? They carry all our heavy artillery. . . ."

"Precisely—and we have to take advantage of that fact!" exclaimed the seneschal, punctuating his words by banging his fist onto the table. "Let's bring our ships up within firing range of the island and pulverize it with our cannon. Then our lighter ships will pass over the chains and our troops can swarm ashore. The island fortifications are not nearly so solid as those of the castle!"

"Bless my soul, now you're talking!" Moruns rumbled and started to smile. "I think that we can take the island. Let's mask our preparations behind fires of damp wood. The wind's in the direction of the Incl positions. If we create a smokescreen, our bombards can easily come within range. . . ."

"That's an excellent idea!" approved the prince as he stroked his short beard. "What do you say, Liane?"

"Tiadann is right! Once the way is free, our ships can sail down the river. We'll leave behind a garrison to continue the siege of the castle, but the greater part of the army can push on to Ronande. If the rog attacks us, he'd better watch out for himself."

This plan was immediately put into execution. The heavy ships anchored before the island under the protection of a thick cloud of smoke, and the bombardment began. Its effects were devastating. The balls rumbled through the air, crumbling the walls of the island fort and creating havoc among its defenders Things went so well that when the men aboard the landing boats came ashore, they met with only sporadic opposition.

By nightfall, the island was in the hands of the Lonks, who made quick work of cutting the strong chains barring passage along the river, so that the ships were able to glide noiselessly downstream.

The occupants of Valiant Castle suspected what was going on and tried to sink the ships with their artillery, but the intense darkness made it impossible for them to adjust their fire, and in the early morning hours as the haze was lifting, they could see in the distance the Lonkian fleet sailing down the river toward the sea . . . Their mission had failed completely; they had counted on immobilizing the Lonk army for many days, but the soldiers had broken through in only a few hours.

The news of this disaster reached Bacdir before he had been able to build up his troop concentrations.

Nevertheless, he had to meet the Lonks in battle lest they cut the roads to the ports and make retreat impossible. It was therefore with a heavy heart that he prepared to confront his adversaries. He had so little confidence in the outcome of the battle that he secretly sent emissaries to the coastal harbors and ordered them to assemble all available ships so that, if necessary, his army could embark for the island of Incl in haste. . . .

"And now what do you say?" trumpeted Tiadann as he and the other army leaders rode through the green Ronande countryside. "Our Incl friends are in for a sorry time. They counted on stopping us at Valiant Castle and here we are on the road to the sea . . ."

"You're a valuable comrade!" Liane affirmed with a big smile. "My voices were right when they told me to have confidence in a stranger who would fight at our side. Now we are going to be able to drive the Incls out of our dear kingdom, and the Lonks will finally know peace! You know, my heart is overwhelmed with sadness when I think of the endless battles we have to fight, but God wills it and we must be bold. Alas, if only Rog Bacdir had been willing to leave our sweet land of Lonk and surrender the noble Duke of Fnar to us. How many lives would be saved . . ."

"Don't count on it, my sweet!" exclaimed Marshal Moruns, who at this moment came riding up at breakneck speed. "The Incls are waiting for us before the good city of Douir, the only important town between our army and the coast. They seem determined to fight, and our forces should be in contact this very evening. What are your orders?"

"By all the saints, Moruns, you have stirred up my

anguish. We will once more have to come to blows with them! Tell me, are there many in the field?"

"To be sure! The rog has called up his first and second lines of reinforcements and our two armies are pretty much equal. However, I've been told that many of his men come from distant southern provinces. The Incls are exhausted and short on supplies. They've had to pillage the surrounding countryside for food."

"Let us go forth boldly!" thundered the Prince of Ardez. "Thanks to the planning of our friend Tiadann, our brave comrades lack for nothing. Our ships will bring all our forces onto the north bank, and then we can go into combat."

"Let's not rush things," the seneschal interjected. "It would be best if we had all our artillery and ammunition supplies with us. The ships are only half a day behind us. Let's wait, so as to be sure that we have everything we need. Then tomorrow, in the early morning, we can confront the Incls under the best possible circumstances. . . ."

This sage counsel was approved by Liane, and the host therefore camped on the banks of the Rifen in a small city that had a large wharf at which the ships could easily dock.

The galactic savant, however, had another reason for acting as he did: he wanted to have exact knowledge of the enemy troop disposition so that he could set up his artillery most advantageously and make the best possible use of his incapacitants. When night fell, therefore, he said he was going out on reconnaissance and set off for a lonely little valley far from prying eyes.

Once there he manipulated the signal key that put him into contact with his spaceship, still in its synchronous orbit, and had it land close by.

His heart thumping with emotion, he entered the navigation cabin, for a short time once more becoming Celsar. The control room reminded him of his faraway country, and for a moment he even thought warmly about Professor Iern'an, languishing in an Aniar jail as he awaited the decision of the ecclesiastical tribunal on the charges of sorcery that had been brought against him. Things would soon come to a head on that matter. . . .

On his planet of origin, Celsar's future had promised to be mediocre; he was only a modest scholar there, whereas here Tiadann was on the road to becoming one of the great in a world that was admittedly primitive, but in many ways more attractive than the well-policed universe he came from. . . .

Without wasting any more time, he activated the protective screen, and programmed the molecular synthesizer to produce large quantities of incapacitants. Tiadann then sat down in front of the navigation controls and the ship was soon in the air, heading toward the north and the Incl encampment.

A few minutes later the immobile and silent spaceship was hovering over the Incl campfires. The infrared viewfinder allowed Tiadann to note the enemy troop dispositions in accurate detail.

Rog Bacdir had established his line on a plain alongside the river. The terrain was broken by numerous thickset hedges—as was the whole region, whose wealth came from its green pastures. Each copse hid archers plentifully supplied with arrows. The numerous streams had been covered over with branches, and many hastily dug ditches awaited the Lonkian horsemen. Under the circumstances, a cavalry charge would have raced to its death: the men, unhorsed, would have found themselves under a rain of arrows once they had broken through the thin ranks of foot-soldiers in the front lines; afterward, the Incl chevaliers massed in the rear would have charged and easily cut the Lonks down.

Tiadann also noted that the enemy artillery had been set up on nearby hills. It therefore dominated the battlefield, and the fleeing masses of Lonks would have been subjected to deadly fire. . . .

The seneschal knew all he had to know. He got up from his observation screen, collected the incapacitants synthesized by his machine, and placed them in special containers that would release a toxic spray on a simple telecommand. Next, Tiadann returned to the navigation cabin and locked these spherical containers into the bomb compartment. Returning then to the controls, he flew over the hills and the rear areas where the Incl knights were massed. All this took only about an hour.

When the last sphere had been dropped over the Incl lines, Tiadann steered the ship toward the valley from which he had departed and disembarked after programming the computer to reposition the spaceship in synchronous orbit.

His horse was waiting for him, peacefully grazing on the rich pasture land. The seneschal mounted, dug in his spurs and regained the Lonkian camp without running into enemy patrols. The cool scented night air made him lose all desire for sleep, so he decided to awaken Ardez and Moruns immediately so that he could set his plans in motion.

Campfires lit up the plain and threw phantasmagoric shadows on the sides of the tents. Here and there, drowsy sentinels leaned on their lances. High in the sky shone the far-off stars from which Tiadann had deliberately cut himself off so that he could live through a marvelous experiment. Only the guard watching over the entrance to the pavilion in which the two Lonkian chiefs slept seemed wide awake; he pointed his lance and demanded that the visitor stand forth and identify himself. Recognizing the seneschal, the guard stepped aside and allowed him to enter the tent.

Tiadann's two friends were sleeping the sleep of the just. Moruns was snoring and sat up with a start when the intruder shook him.

"Great balls of fire!" he swore. "You frightened the hell out of me . . . What's happening? Are the Incls attacking?"

"Not at all! I simply came to give you some interesting news. . . ."

Ardez in turn grumblingly extricated himself from his blankets, energetically scratched his head, and soon seemed clear-minded enough to listen to what the seneschal had to say.

"Here's how things stand," said the latter. "I've made a little night reconnaissance and that has given me an idea of the battle dispositions of the Incl troops."

"Fascinating!" exclaimed the duke. "That's a bold thing to do—make a trip across enemy lines all by yourself."

"Bah! Those accursed dogs were sleeping soundly," said Tiadann lightly. "They seemed exhausted, and thunder itself wouldn't have awakened them!"

"Speak, Good God!" roared the fiery marshal. "You must have learned something important enough to have made you rouse us out of our beds!"

"I think I have! . . . The enemy artillery is dug in on the hills. In addition, the Incls have sown the plain with traps that are sure to unseat our horsemen. Once that's done, their crossbows and harquebuses need only fire into the pile of floundering knights. I'm convinced that any mass attack is doomed to certain failure."

"Well, what do you suggest?" mumbled Ardez, yawning widely enough to throw his jaws out of joint.

"We have to counteract the fire of their bombards by placing our artillery pieces on the cliffs over on our right wing."

"Hell and damnation, my friend! You really go at it . . ." objected the bastard. "We would never have time enough to do that!"

"I don't agree with you! Let's yoke the oxen to the bombards, and attach straw to the wheels to muffle the noise. By dawn, everything will be in place."

"What do you think, Ardez?" asked Moruns.

"Damn it, if Tiadann says it's possible . . . It won't be light until six. We still have eight hours. It can be done . . ."

"And how will we find our way in the darkness?"

"I'll take care of that," Tiadann assured him. "I've already spotted a few paths that seem possible, and I can be the convoy guide. . . ."

"No doubt about it—you're a valuable man to have around," said Moruns admiringly. "Should we talk to Liane about this?"

"There's no reason to. The important thing is that she be fit tomorrow and that her banner be seen waving in the front ranks of our army. Let her sleep in peace."

"You're right," approved the marshal. "Without Liane, the men would be lost! Wake our people. We'll get into our armor and join you near the artillery pieces."

Tiadann went quietly off to prepare everything. When the lieutenant general and the marshal rejoined him, the men who manned the artillery pieces were already yoking up the oxen, working in absolute silence. Eventually, there was a long line of guns and heavily loaded ammunition wagons, their wheels muffled with straw, the entire operation carried out by the light of the flickering campfires alone, with only a few stifled curses occasionally breaking the silence.

Finally, the convoy started up toward the neighboring heights; the initial creaking of badly greased wheels was quickly smothered. At the head of the column was Tiadann; seated on his robust chestnut steed, he discreetly consulted his infrared viewfinder in order to choose the best road. Everything went off as he had planned.

By dawn the heavy bombards had been set up in a battery. Nearby, the gunners were stirring the glowing embers that would be used to light the wicks. The lieutenant general, the marshal, and the seneschal had already redescended to the plain and were urging their men into battle formation. All three felt astonishingly fresh and rested. (It should be pointed out that Tiadann had made them drink a few swallows of a powerful stimulant mixed into the wine in his gourd. . . .)

On their side the Incls were by no means inactive; the foot soldiers massing in the plain seemed a tempting prey for the Lonkian chevaliers, whose Incl peers remained sagely in the rear according to the established battle plan.

Liane had already taken her place at the head of her troops. She looked fine astride her white palfrey, her banner flapping in the wind. Following Tiadann's orders, Moruns and Ardez remained at her side in order to restrain her impetuousness.

As for the seneschal, he had repositioned himself near the bombards carefully hidden on the hill, so that he would later be able to direct their fire by making radio contact with the viewfinder surveying the enemy positions from his spaceship.

When the two armies were ranged in battle formation, the Maid waved her banner several times as a signal for the Lonkian knights to launch the attack. One after another, the heavy squadrons started up amid the whinnying of horses and the thunder of hooves beating against the ground.

The Incls let them come on; when they were within range, the first ranks retreated hastily, but in good order, so that the enemy cavalry would fall into the traps prepared for them. Unfortunately for the Incls, Moruns and Ardez made a rapid about-face and turned back. Behind them the Lonkian infantry moved in serried ranks toward the Incls.

Soon the foot soldiers were engaged in combat. The Incls let fly with their crossbows and the Lonks replied with their harquebuses. The projectiles caused an equal number of fatalities on both sides. Then the hand-to-hand fighting began.

Tiadann chose this moment to unmask his batteries. He had carefully verified the vertical sighting of the bombards, but now he fired four of the pieces to adjust their range. After a few modifications had been made, he ordered sustained and rapid fire. The Incls were completely unprepared for such an attack, and their artillery was pointed toward the plain. As a result, the Lonkian cannonballs wreaked havoc among the Incls before they could reply to Tiadann's artillery with even a few sporadic shots.

It was too late. . . . Almost all the heavy iron cannon soon lay on the ground, surrounded by the bodies of the gunners. The overturned linstocks started a brush fire, and before long the powder wagons began to explode; panic reigned. During all this, the infantry continued methodically gutting one another on the plain, while behind them the chevaliers passively watched the spectacle as their horses impatiently pawed the ground.

At that moment, Tiadann grabbed for his telecommand apparatus and caused the containers filled with incapacitants to explode. The Incl horses and horsemen inhaled a strong dose of the light ochre-colored smoke that rose from the thick grass. As though in a dream, the sturdy steeds could be seen luxuriously stretching themselves in the meadows; the Incl knights, imprisoned in their suits of iron, were sprawled on the ground like so many overturned turtles, unable to right themselves.

Seizing a scarlet banner, Tiadann waved it twice. Immediately the Lonkian horsemen started forward in tight formation, but instead of riding straight toward their enemies, they climbed the hills on which no traps had been dug, since the Incls had counted on their artillery to protect their flank.

Liane at their head, the cavalry troops reached the rear of the infantry; turning left, they charged down the slopes at top speed. Just then something completely unexpected happened. Tiadann had forgotten to consult his meteorological computer. . . . The black clouds that filled the inky sky suddenly broke, and cataracts of rain fell on the battlefield, dispersing the aerosol incapacitants under sheets of water. If the downpour had occurred a few minutes earlier, Tiadann's plan would have failed. As it happened, the rain did not cause any major catastrophe. A few steeds, their four iron shoes sliding along the damp ground of the fields, stumbled and unseated their horsemen, but most of the Lonks reached the Incl knights, who were still immobilized on the ground.

The long Lonkian lances brought carnage—actually a useless slaughter, since the brave warriors could not have harmed so much as a fly! Such are the horrors of war. . . .

Meanwhile, the Incl infantry, hearing the shouts behind it, became aware of its plight and there was an indescribable rout. Half the men tried to flee toward the river; the others climbed the hills toward their silenced and completely incapacitated artillery. Those who had chosen the hills managed to escape. Rejoining those gunners who were still alive, they fled north without further ado. The wretches who had sought salvation on the riverbank found themselves trapped between the Lonkian cavalry and infantry. A few tried to put up a desperate struggle; the others jumped into the water and were drowned. Finally, horrified by the spectacle, Liane had the trumpets sounded and put an end to the massacre.

The day had been well spent; the Lonks had gained an overwhelming victory. All of the invaders' artillery had been captured, and two-thirds of its infantry taken prisoner or put to the sword. As for the arrogant knights who had for years caused a reign of terror in the kingdom, less than a dozen had escaped. Among them was Bacdir; haggard and worn, he had barely been rescued by a few of his men, who hastily hoisted him atop a horse that had managed to remain on its feet.

The rest of the host made a forced march toward the ports on the coast. Henceforth, the kingdom of Lonk was free; the hard-pressed and disgraced invader had turned tail and gone home. . . .

Chapter Four

Liane remained on the battlefield until nightfall. The rain was still coming down in sheets, forming a bog of mud and blood, but she continued to treat the wounded, bandaging them and trying to ease their suffering. Even the dying regained a bit of strength at the sight of her.

The Maid had a word of comfort for each. Tears coursed down her noble face and she was completely indifferent to the rain that soaked her to the skin. Never had she been able to accustom herself to the battles she had to wage, and each time she regretted that the deliverance of the sweet kingdom of Lonk had to be paid for with so much pain and so many tears.

Tiadann accompanied her. He had brought with him painkilling medicines that he administered to those most sorely wounded, and he was profoundly sorry that he did not have a more abundant therapeutic arsenal.

As for Moruns and Ardez, they followed on the heels of the Incls, while the uninjured Lonks who had survived the battle busily assembled the considerable booty abandoned by the vanquished.

When evening came, Liane and Tiadann fell into a leaden sleep. The galactic scholar tossed uneasily, ceaselessly going over in his mind the best way to turn the course of events to his advantage. He wanted to become so famous and indispensable that Sranz could not do without him. To accomplish this, he would have to make some improvements in the local technology. The artillery, despite his modifications, was still far from being reliable. During the last battle the rain had soaked the matchlocks and interfered with the harquebus fire. A new percussion system had to be worked out.

He also had to give some thought to a fleet that would allow the Lonkian host to disembark on the island of the Incls. Here, too, existing techniques would have to be considerably improved. If his plans were to be carried out successfully, he needed Liane's complete support, which is why he decided on a new ruse. His spaceship contained an extremely efficient hypnosuggester: if he were to use it on Liane, her dreams could be made to conform to his desires. He therefore left the camp once more and went to get this precious instrument.

That done, he programmed it to make the Archangel Lignel appear in Liane's dreams, hoping that the montages he prepared would be sufficiently like the Maid's usual visions to convince her.

In the morning, Liane's face was serene and rested. "Last night my celestial visitors came back to see me," she announced to Tiadann. "They were very pleased with my conduct: I've liberated the kingdom and had Sranz crowned, but they say my mission is still not over. The good Duke of Fnar remains a prisoner! 'Liane,' Lignel and the powers accompanying him order me, 'you must now go to free the gentle duke! However, don't undertake such an operation lightly. First you are to move the Lonkian host against the

Duke of Xovia so that his troops cannot occupy the kingdom while you are making war beyond the seas. The valiant Moruns and Ardez will aid you in this task. While they are thus occupied, you will turn preparations for the seaborne invasion over to Tiadann. This stranger is skillful in the arts of war. He will forge the arms you need for victory. Rely on him completely. He deserves your full confidence.' "

"Such praise embarrasses me," said the seneschal modestly. "It is true, however, that I am completely devoted to both the Lonkian cause and to the Maid of Fnar! I will try to prove myself worthy of this confidence. . . . I will set about preparing the artillery and the ships. When the royal army returns in triumph, everything will be ready for it to cross the channel."

"My great thanks for your loyalty, faithful Tiadann. I can guarantee that the king will know how to reward your merits when the time comes!"

Greatly pleased with having fooled the gentle Maid, the seneschal bowed from the waist. There was no doubt about it, things were decidedly working out very well for him. . . .

Liane returned to the capital in order to convince King Sranz to attack the Xovians. As soon as Ronande had been completely pacified, Ardez and Moruns rejoined her there with the greater part of the army.

Rog Bacdir had succeeded in returning to his island with a few Incl companies that had hastily been embarked onto those ships he had taken the precaution to keep in readiness at the ports.

An enormous amount of booty fell to the Lonks; the most precious part, as Tiadann saw it, was an arsenal of cannon that he had every intention of using against those who had manufactured them.

The scholar had also quit the battlefield, but though

Valiant Castle had surrendered and the river was once more open, he didn't return to the capital. He decided there was no point in moving his artillery because later on he would only have to transfer it to the port towns on the coast.

Douir had excellent craftsmen and foundries that were eminently capable of making the improvements Tiadann had in mind. Olmuth, the venerable chief of the blacksmith's guild, undertook to furnish him with workers and workshops. What Tiadann wanted most of all was a dependable material. The matchlock with the worm that drove the incandescent point onto the pan had been a significant improvement, but it wasn't enough. The climate of the island of the Incls was very damp, and the fuse, even if it were impregnated with saltpeter, might still go out; standing in the skillful artisan's smithy, the seneschal explained to Olmuth what was needed. Nearby glowed a wood fire fanned by young apprentices working an enormous leather bellows; the reflection of the embers made the faces of both men seem purple, and sweat flowed down their cheeks.

"What we have to do, Olmuth, is adapt to portable arms a completely sealed mechanism that can always be depended upon to set off the powder charge. In my far-off country we have substances or alloys that send off sparks when struck. Do you know of any similar materials here?"

"Let's see now," said the smith, screwing up his craggy face. "There are those crystals that people call fool's gold. Sometimes you find little balls of them that look like animal droppings. . . ."

"Pyrites," exclaimed Tiadann. "Perfect! I had considered using silex, but your fool's gold will do just as well if you can get a large enough supply."

"There's none in our region. Generally, fool's gold is found in the east, but on the other hand, silex is just about everywhere."

"Fine! In that case we'll use silex. Now let me have a piece of chalk so that I can make you a sketch of a wheel lock. . . ."

An apprentice brought some chalk, and the seneschal drew on the floor of the smithy a diagram of the mechanism he wanted made. As he filled in his sketch, he offered some explanations.

"This lock can be used on light portable arms with short barrels—let's just call them pistols—as well as on long-barreled weapons that are more precise. On top is a pistol hammer, which when pulled back compresses a spring and pin in such a way that the tensed spring is caught in a notch. At that point the weapon is cocked, in other words ready to fire. All you have to do is press down on the trigger. The spring pushes forward the hammer, which strikes the silex and loosens a spray of sparks. These sparks bring the fire to the powder heaped in the barrel, and the shot goes off without fail!"

"By heaven! that's a cunning little contraption, and no doubt about it! But doesn't it break down easily?"

"Not at all! If you use a good alloy—I'll show you how it's made up—the spring will always drive the hammer forward, and since the entire mechanism is inside the weapon, it's protected against the damp. . . ."

"I get it! That's damned clever—I would never have been able to think up something like that!"

"You've probably also realized that there's no reason not to give the weapons several superimposed barrels, each of which could have its own flintlock. That way, you can have as many as four charges for each gun. . . ."

"Great God! With weapons like this in our hands, the Incls had better start counting their dead! If every Lonk soldier kills four Incls, there soon won't be any left on that island of theirs! Still," he added after a moment of reflection, "I wonder if it's really a good thing. . . . Under these conditions war would become impossible—there'd be too many dead!"

"And another thing," continued Tiadann, ignoring the objection. "These guns will shoot iron balls of a fair size. That means that the aiming will have to be accurate. The best thing would be for you to mount a little pointer on the end of the barrel and attach a small plate with a hole in it on the breech. By putting his eye to the hole, the gunner will be able to aim at his man with precision."

"Great balls of fire! How did you ever think that up? It's simple enough, of course, but the thing is to have thought of it. You've certainly got a head on you, there's no doubt about it," enthused the old man, in a tone that showed how impressed he was.

Pleased by the compliment, Tiadann continued in a casual manner: "Oh, we know a lot more tricks than that where I come from! For example, suppose you wanted to hit several enemies at a time with a single shot from a single gun. What would you do?"

"Why, I can't begin to im—"

"All you have to do is widen the end of the barrel and load it with metal pellets instead of a ball. When you do that, there's a dispersion of projectiles that can hit several of the enemy grouped in one spot."

"Thunderation! I'd never have thought it possible. . . . But I'm sure you're right, seneschal. That Maid certainly knows how to choose her people!" the smith exclaimed in admiring tones.

"All right, now let's consider the bombards. They'll

have to be set up on the ships and ready for use, because you can be sure the Incls will try to intercept our fleet. Toothed racks will allow them to be trained vertically, and that's better than nothing. But I want them to be able to fire on the coast from directions other than the one the ship is moving in. Do you see what I mean?"

"Of course! The Incls will never suspect a thing if one of our ships presents its flank."

"Exactly! Of course we could position our bombards perpendicular to the sheathing and planking, but then the bows would be unarmed."

"That's a fine idea, but the carriages are devilishly heavy. . . . How are we going to turn them?"

"Simple! We'll mount them on circular plaques sunk into the deck. These supports will rest on iron balls placed in ring-shaped grooves. The spheres will move on a circular disk so that the friction will be cut down. Do you think you can manufacture something like that?"

"No problem, seneschal. With all due respect, I have to say that you've really got it up there," said the smith, rapping a finger against his forehead.

"Come now!" protested Tiadann. "All I've done is make a few suggestions. I'm sure that all these things have been buzzing around in your head for quite a while."

Saying this, he directed toward the smith the beam of a psycho-suggester he had in his pocket. The truth was that the scientist was in no way eager to have his name directly associated with all the improvements made by the Lonks. Nor did he want to have local science progress too rapidly—as it would, for example, if he taught the good smith to make revolvers that used percussion bullets. On the other hand, the Imperial inspectors wouldn't find these modifications of the aborigines' firearms strange: everything he had ordered the smith to do was well within the basic technology of the epoch. One day or another, some clever artisan would have hit upon these modifications. If he covered his tracks, his presence on the planet would not be suspected, and he would have time enough to shape this civilization as he wanted to.

While Tiadann was thinking all this, the good Olmuth had remained mute, as though paralyzed, but then his features regained their normal animation and he said:

"I don't want to boast, but I actually have been thinking about all these improvements for some time. It's just that I didn't have enough money to work them out, that's all. Thanks to you, sir, that part's easy now, and I'm very grateful."

"It's nothing, nothing at all, my friend. All I ask is that you do your work well. Here, suppose you take these gold pieces on account. You can have more after you deliver the first turret gear and some percussion guns."

"May God bless you! And don't worry, I'll see to it that things get moving." Upon which, the exchange ended, and the two parties withdrew, each extremely satisfied with the other.

But Tiadann was by no means through. Douir was an important shipbuilding city as well, and the seneschal also wanted to make a small contribution to the new ships that would be used for the invasion. To do this he used the same method of suggestion on the master of the guild of carpenters who specialized in maritime construction. It was in this manner that the crafty scientist led the Lonks to construct landing barges whose bows could be lowered to form gangways from which the horses could descend once the boat had been beached.

He also made some rudder modifications. Until then, the helmsmen had worked the helm with the aid of pulley blocks. Tiadann suggested the installation of manual tillers with a relay; in this way one could keep an eye on the sails as one steered. He also had the Lonks increase the size of the rudder blade as well as of the helm's angle of rotation, so that overall efficiency was improved: a ship could now be brought about sharply without the help of the sails.

The seneschal also wanted to make some changes in the rigging. Generally speaking, the ships did not have fore or mizzen masts. Their one square sail was difficult to handle and didn't allow for sailing close to the wind. The addition of a spanker sail aft and a mizzen sail fore considerably improved maneuverability. The rigging also left much to be desired because sail lines were held by pulleys. Tiadann advised that they be attached to channels by deadeyes and lanyards. Similarly, the shape of the poop was modified, becoming decidedly square.

Because he wanted to facilitate the aiming of the artillery, Tiadann gave orders that the ships were to be made very sturdy and have reinforced ribs and decks. The mizzen mast of these galliots was eliminated and replaced by jibs during navigation. When the enemy drew near, the jibs were taken in, thereby enabling the heavy bombards mounted on the new revolving carriages to be aimed. The angle of departure could be as much as ninety degrees. On some of the ships a turret would be mounted in front of the mizzen mast. Other cannon would be placed before large portholes, which allowed for a forty-five-degree orientation.

When all this was done, the Lonkian fleet would

not only be able to maneuver efficiently, but the guns could be trained on the enemy without first bringing the ship into a head-on position.

Another change was that sturdy gunwales were built above the planking so that the crew would be protected from the crossbow arrows; a hoist brought sacks of ammunition to the marksmen installed in the tops. None of these modifications were especially revolutionary, either, and they were completely compatible with the technology of the time: no Imperial inspector would find them unusual. Technical advances always came in sudden leaps and were followed by a period of stabilization.

The master of the shipyards was also made to think that he had initiated all these improvements and that the seneschal had merely furnished him with the money he needed to carry out ideas he had been thinking of for years but had been unable to put into practice until now.

His mission accomplished, Tiadann left Douir and returned to the capital. He wanted to make sure that Sranz was still under his influence and that there was no chance of anything going wrong. He also wanted to be present at the trial of his compatriot, Alterdo, who was soon to be judged by an ecclesiastic tribunal. Though he felt no pity for him, he was eager to make sure that the unfortunate wretch had the chance to remain alive—a concept which his race understood as the inhabitants of Noldaz did not.

A messenger had informed him that the trial would begin in about ten days; there was therefore time enough to sail tranquilly up the river aboard one of the ships linking Douir with Aniar.

Drawn by sturdy teams of oxen, Tiadann's small boat serenely mounted the course of the Rifen, allowing him leisure enough to consider the situation while he watched the greenish waters flow slowly past the mossy flanks of the barge.

The outcome of the final reckoning between the Lonks and the Xovians was certain; Moruns and Ardez would know how best to advise Liane, and the host would return victorious before two months were up. Bacdir would no doubt profit from this period to raise a new army and to assemble all the navigable Incl ships in order to fight off the invasion, but this could in no way change anything. The Lonkian fleet, armed as it was with rotatable bombards and capable of maneuvering with considerably greater ease than before, would certainly manage to make the channel crossing successfully.

The land battle would probably be favorable to the Lonks, but there was no point in underestimating the enemy; just in case, it would be better to make use of the incapacitants—weather permitting, of course. They could, however, only be used in a limited way: if the Incls all drowsed off on the battlefield, the fact would surely be noted and might very well draw the attention of the Imperial inspectors.

Later . . . well, later Sranz would name a regent of the Incl island; this would be tantamount to an absolute monarchy over the two kingdoms, and since the king was no more than a puppet manipulated by Tiadann . . .

In a way, Tiadann would have liked to have had Alterdo witness his rise to power, because a success that is not observed by somebody capable of appreciating it is less interesting.

With the arsenal of drugs he had at his disposal, Tiadann could easily have obtained Alterdo's acquittal . . . Alas, if he did that he would once again have to put up with the professor's everlasting warnings! And after all, who was Alterdo? An unimaginative nobody who couldn't bear the application of the experimental method to history and who was always in a sweat about the Imperial inspectors even though they were completely overwhelmed by the task of surveillance over billions of planets!

For a long time Tiadann weighed the pros and cons. When he got to Aniar, he had still not made up his mind and finally decided to follow his inspiration.

His first visit, of course, was to Sranz who gave him a warm welcome and lavished on him praise and presents. He informed the king that the operations against Xovia had begun and were going nicely. Sranz was still under his seneschal's influence and approved all his decisions, so there was no problem in that area. He even spoke to Tiadann about his compatriot and assured him that he was quite ready to intervene in Alterdo's favor. The seneschal shrugged off this suggestion, declaring that he wouldn't think of asking for special favors if Alterdo was indeed guilty of serious crimes and that he would rely completely on the judgment of the tribunal. All he asked for was permission to visit his friend. This granted, Tiadann went off to see the prisoner in his cell, which was situated in the cellars of the chateau of Aniar's archimandrite. The royal pass with which he was armed opened all doors, and he soon gained entrance to the squalid, damp-walled dungeon in which Alterdo had been chained for the past few months.

In the dark, he could just barely make out the prisoner's face. The professor hadn't changed very much. His features were emaciated, and his general thinness showed that he didn't always eat his fill, but his eyes, sunk in their deep cavities, still had the same alertness. This was no surprise since his human phenotype merely sheltered a diaphanous being composed of atomic plasma and drawing its strength exclusively from planetary magnetic fields. Contrary to what Tiadann expected, his ex-colleague did not heap abuse on him. After studying him in silence for a moment, he exclaimed:

"You're looking fine, you old rascal! Apparently you're having no difficulty adapting yourself to your human condition. . . . So you've finally decided to pay me a visit. Very thoughtful of you! Given everything that's happened on this planet, I've had plenty to think about, but I'd like to have a few precise details from you–my jailers tend to be rather thick-headed, and there's not much to be gotten out of them. Have you managed to defeat the Incls and free the kingdom of Lonk?"

"Of course! The program Liane set herself has just about been completed: the king has been crowned, he reigns in his capital, and we've beaten the Incls hollow. I'm planning an invasion of their island just as soon as the Prince of Ardez and Marshal Moruns have defeated the Duke of Xovia. Once that's done, we won't have to worry about being attacked from the rear."

"A well-thought-out plan, my dear seneschal–I've heard you've been named to that exalted rank. Will you be the one to judge me?"

"No, I'll merely be called as a witness at your trial. To tell the truth, I don't mix much in matters of justice: I'm mainly the Lonkian war leader and I'm a member of the council that decides on military operations. I've also got a hand in logistics. . . ."

"Naturally! You must have really outsmarted this band of idiots. It's as plain as can be that by manipulating the Maid and the king you're the one who really rules the kingdom. . . ."

"There's no keeping anything from you! But don't give me away," bantered Tiadann with a sly smile. "Nobody even suspects my magic powers."

"Bah! Who would believe me? I'm trapped in this envelope of flesh. I've lost almost all my powers except those for telepathy, and since you carefully mask your thoughts, even they don't do me any good. Would you at least be kind enough to let me know what you're planning to do? I have to admit I can't begin to imagine why you want to rule these primitives. Of course, your theories confuting cyclical history have been confirmed. I've thought about that quite a bit, and there's no doubt but that the influence of local culture, the state, and religion are significant. You know how to draw on these factors and you seem to have been able to prevent the decline of your heroine! Fine! You've won: history cannot be entirely foreseen with the aid of computers and probability factors—at least so long as the innumerable facts that enter into play are not known down to their smallest details. But the more I think about it, the less I can see what it is you want to accomplish. . . ."

"You're a good sport! Thanks for admitting your errors. In return, I'll put my cards on the table. What would have happened to this planct if it had followed the Imperial galactic norms?"

"Why, its evolution would have been quite ordinary: states would have developed, people would have become aware of the concept of nations, then monarchic governments would have been replaced first by dictatorships and later by democratic republics."

"Exactly! And that's just what I want to avoid."

"But why? All humanoid peoples go through these different phases. . . ."

"Precisely: nations are born, tear each other to pieces over territorial questions, and there are incessant wars until the day when one of the adversaries discovers the power of the atom. Then, if moral and philosophic evolution has not kept up with the physical sciences—genocide."

"They get what they deserve! Nothing forces them to kill one another off!" exclaimed Alterdo.

"Well, my friend, I feel that the Imperial inspectors ought to prevent all this instead of remaining simple spectators! And that's why I've decided to spare the inhabitants of this planet these trials. I want to unify all the peoples, impose a common language, establish a Federal Union of Nations. I'm going to occupy the island of the Incls and try my first experiment on it. I'll have myself named regent and set up schools in which all Incls will learn to speak Lonkian. The same goes for Xovia. Then I'll establish a single government over the entire continent. Afterward, I'll send an expedition overseas to occupy the vast and rich virgin territories that are only waiting for me to discover them. The primitive peoples who live there will also be taught to speak Lonkian. By doing this, I can spare Noldaz the horrors of war, and its evolution will be considerably accelerated. Nobody has ever dared to modify the normal course of history so radically, but I intend to do so, and the Imperial inspectors will find themselves faced with a *fait accompli!*"

"Galaxy!" exclaimed the professor in amazement. "You've ambitious plans. . . . Of course, they're utopian, but they're also fascinating! Why didn't you tell me about them sooner? I could have helped you. . . ."

"Come now, my friend, don't take me for an idiot!

You haven't got the stomach for my sort of approach. The very mention of the Imperial inspectors paralyzed you. I couldn't take a chance!"

"Maybe you're right . . . I prefer not to be mixed up in this madness. But tell me something. To have gained this kind of victory over the Incls you must have seriously contravened our laws and accelerated local technological development considerably. But you haven't made use of atomic weapons, have you?"

"Of course not! All I did was provide the Lonkian army with a few improvements. Though they're still quite primitive, their artillery and fleet completely outclass those of the Incls. I've also made limited use of incapacitants. Trust me, I've been careful: I defy any inspector to spot an anachronism on this planet. You know, sometimes just a little thing can make the balance shift in favor of an army."

"So you want to become emperor of this world. . . . Your talk is respectable enough, but aren't you likely to fall victim to ambition? Your role doesn't seem to displease you—far from it!—and you're hungry for power. . . ."

"That's my business. Don't believe me if you don't want to. In any case, you can't deny that thanks to me the natives of this planet will be spared much useless suffering."

"We shall see. . . . And now let's talk about me. What are your plans for my humble self?"

"You cannot be my ally, and I'm not eager to have you go off and tell foolish stories to Liane and Sranz. I've therefore decided to let your trial run its course."

"In other words, I'm to be condemned to burn at the stake as a heretic and a sorcerer!"

"Exactly! In that way you'll be forced to quit your envelope of flesh and become Iern'an once more. A sphere of luminiscent plasma would only terrify these humanoids, so you won't be able to interfere with my plans."

"Will you at least permit me to go back to our spaceship?"

"You must be joking! The first thing you would do would be to send out a distress signal! No, Iern'an–but I'll see to it that you have everything you need to survive and not be too bored. Don't count on Imperial aid. Nobody knows that we're here, and we're practically immortal. Under the circumstances, the future belongs to me!"

"Nevertheless, Celsar, you might have spared me the burning; it will be an uncomfortable moment to go through."

"Oh, come now! All you have to do is shut off the connections with the sensory system of your human body. You won't feel a thing. . . ."

"And what will people say when they see me appear above the flames and rise into the sky?"

"Everybody there will be convinced that you really were a servant of Satan, and they'll swear that the devil personally carried off your soul."

"What an unpleasant fellow you are!" sighed the unfortunate professor. "Well, I can see that you've thought of everything. There's no use of further discussion as I'll never convince you of your folly. I've a feeling that all this will end badly. Once I'm free, can I at least have a few psychic reels so that I can continue my studies?"

"Of course! And if you need regeneration sessions, just let me know. The planet's magnetic field is fairly powerful, but one never knows, and I don't want you to suffer unnecessarily, Iern'an. All I want to do is prevent you from interfering with my plans."

"You're too kind!" grumbled the professor. "Tell me, am I to languish in this pigsty much longer? Please do what you can to speed up my trial."

"It will begin tomorrow. Don't confess immediately, but don't deny things too long. If you do as I say, you'll avoid torture. Who knows—your control over your neurons may not be as good as you think it is."

"Thanks for the advice, my loyal friend. . . . Well, I guess there's nothing more to say. We'll meet again tomorrow," concluded the professor with an ambiguous smile.

Tiadann departed, satisfied with having avoided a disagreeable scene. However, he couldn't help wondering why the professor had seemed so resigned. . . . He would have liked to undertake a psychic probing of his former friend, but of course, like himself, the professor had set up a psychic barrier that prevented all telepathic communication.

Shrugging his shoulders, Tiadann gave up the idea of trying to understand Iern'an's motives. After all, perhaps the professor had simply decided to take things easy, since there was nothing he could do to oppose the ambitious plans of his former assistant.

As for the stake, that was a mere formality designed to satisfy the natives; his race had total control over the temporarily assumed fleshly disguise, so Iern'an would never feel a moment's pain. Satisfied, the seneschal left the prison and returned to his comfortable room in the palace. In it he found a delightful chambermaid who enjoyed his favors, and freeing his neurons, he spent a few very pleasant moments. . . .

Chapter Five

The castle's royal chapel was filled to capacity. Lords, burghers and noble ladies accompanied by their pages had all come to see this rather unusual spectacle: the trial of a sorcerer. Tiadann, as seneschal of the kingdom, had the right to an armchair in the front row of spectators.

The ecclesiastic tribunal was seated in a semi-circle at the center of which the archimandrite, dressed in robes of gold, sat in state on a raised cathedra. Before them was a wooden bench reserved for the accused, and near it were clerks seated behind a table covered with green cloth.

In addition to the archimandrite, there were six other judges: the prosecutor, the venerable and discreet Counselor Orvell; Tivet, the exorcist and specialist in canon law; and various doctors and professors of theology—abbots and priors. A court usher assisted them.

Alterdo was brought into the chapel by ten pike-bearing guards who took up positions along the center aisle. The accused had been permitted his richest finery, so in spite of his pallor, he looked extremely impressive. Alterdo stood straight and took advantage of every inch of his height; his eagle's glance proudly swept over his judges, and he showed deep contempt for these primitives. A slight smile appeared on his lips, and it was quite easy for Tiadann to see that the professor was thinking bitterly of the ridiculousness of his situation.

And, in truth, these lowly humanoids would have had no chance at all against him if he had been able to get his hands on some of the instruments in the spaceship that was even now in orbit high in the sky above the palace. Only the disloyalty of his compatriot made it possible for these ludicrous and pretentious primitives to pass judgment on a member of the Galactic Empire; even so they were in reality completely incapable of doing him the least harm, for his real body—hidden in his envelope of flesh—was incredibly resistant, and insensitive to both the sword and the flame.

After having gazed at the accused in silence, as though to gauge his capabilities, the president of the tribunal declared in a hollow voice:

"This insolent man before you has been imprisoned on the request of the noble Tiadann, seneschal of the kingdom. The charge against him is one of the most serious; sorcery. Our most serene and mighty Sranz VII has granted us power to conduct his trial and therefore he has been called to appear before us. Accused, swear on our Holy Books to tell the truth, the whole truth, in answer to the questions we shall put to you. . . ."

Alterdo sneered bitterly, accentuating his sarcastic smile and he said in a scathing tone:

"Your so-called holy books are just about good enough for use in the privy. Such being the case, I don't see why I should take the oath, since it wouldn't keep me from telling you anything I felt like saying."

A horrified murmur ran through the spectators, and

the archimandrite himself seemed terrified by such sacrilege. Finally he pointed a stern finger at the accused and exclaimed: "You are possessed by the devil! How else can your impious words be explained? I call on you to make honorable amends!"

"Go screw yourself!"

"Enough!" said the president, turning toward his assessors. "You can see for yourselves, gentlemen, how completely this unfortunate creature is under the power of the forces of evil. Keep it in mind when you render your sentence. Let us continue. What is your name?"

"Alterdo Zanzini—at least that's how I'm known here."

"Does that mean you have other names? The Prince of Darkness has undoubtedly given you a secret name that you are sworn not to reveal."

"Stop raving, you old imbecile! Elsewhere I'm called Iern'an."

"And may not this 'elsewhere' be the dwelling place of the infernal spirits?"

"Don't knock yourself out—there's no way for you to understand."

"You refuse to recognize the authority of the court before which you stand?"

"I simply mean that your learning is insufficient to enable you to understand my origin. I come from another world. . . ."

"Nonsense! As though there were worlds other than our own—except of course from the Empyrean and the dwelling place of the damned. Don't start lying, Alterdo—our patience is exhausted! I suppose there's no point in asking if you follow the practices of our Holy Religion?"

"Why should I? I'm rather too highly evolved to show interest in your children's games!"

"Another insult! Fine! I can see that evil is deeply rooted in you. Let's go on to the charges against you. Do you know who your parents are?"

"Better than you know who yours are!"

"Might you not perhaps be born of an incubus or succubus? Weren't you promised to the Evil One from the very moment of your birth?"

"Do stop talking nonsense."

"So you don't deny it! The tribunal will know how to interpret that . . . Is it true that you have privately received noble lords and ladies to whom you foretold the future?"

"This time my answer is yes, and I don't think any of my visitors can complain about my divinations."

"Precisely! How can you know about events that have not yet happened unless you make use of demonic practices? Everyone knows that only God presides over the destinies of his creatures and the universe."

"To be completely truthful, I don't really deal with certainties but with high degrees of probability."

"What do you mean by that?"

"I tell you once more that you are far too ignorant to understand these phenomena."

"Strange: we represent the highest ecclesiastical authorities in the kingdom, and you claim that we are too ignorant! Is there no limit to your pride? Or is it perhaps that the demon you harbor is befuddling your senses! Let us continue. . . . Have you given liquors and philters designed to bring success in matters of love to those who have come to you for help?"

"I don't deny it."

"Can you give us the formula?"

"Obviously not!"

"In other words, these are demonic practices—drugs compounded according to satanic precepts, to methods so foul that you dare not reveal them!"

"Come now, I defy you to prove that. Nobody has suffered from them, and all I've done is make products formulated according to the most rigorous laws of science."

"Can you furnish any proof of what you are saying?"

"Next question!"

"So you admit that you are a sorcerer? A necromancer who by heretical practices has tried to enrich himself as a result of a pact with the devil?"

Alterdo shrugged his shoulders without replying.

The archimandrite insisted: "There's no use playing for time: have I or haven't I stated the truth?"

"Your foolishness is beginning to bore me. Ask Tiadann what he thinks of all this."

"It is precisely our intention to question the noble seneschal who knew you so well—and who, given your diabolical practices, thought it best to ask for your imprisonment. Usher, call forth the witness."

Preceded by a guard, Tiadann came to stand before the tribunal, and the president continued:

"Sir Seneschal, please take the oath on our Holy Books."

The usher presented the sacred volumes and Tiadann pronounced the accepted formula:

"Before God who is my witness and on these Holy Books I swear to tell the truth, the whole truth, and nothing but the truth."

"Perfect!" cackled the president, and then continued in an unctuous tone: "It is obvious, noble sir, that you respect the precepts of our Holy Religion. Tell me, have you known the accused for a long time?"

"Yes, of course. But I might add that he has only recently begun to indulge in satanic practices."

"Did you know his parents?"

"No. . . ."

"Then you cannot deny that at the moment of his birth Alterdo was consecrated to the devil."

"I know nothing about that."

"Very well. The tribunal will make note of the reply. Have you yourself noticed that the accused was indulging in necromantic divination and that he would compound malevolent drugs in some secret laboratory?"

"That's the very reason I asked for his arrest. I feared that this person represented a danger to our co-citizens, whose good faith he abused by his fallacious practices."

"The tribunal thanks you for your vigilance, noble seneschal. As for myself, I have already come to a decision. Do any of my assessors wish to ask the witness additional questions?"

"Yes," said the exorcist, rising to his feet.

"Please proceed, Exorcist Tivet. . . ."

"Does the seneschal have any notion of where the accused comes from and whether or not he might be in the pay of the Incls?"

"A judicious question. What is your reply, noble sir?"

"I couldn't really say that is so, but in his conversations with me, this Zanzini made no attempt to hide his sympathies for them. He didn't want the Maid to continue her exploits. According to him, sooner or later she was to be abandoned by all and die a terrible death."

"Are you satisfied, Exorcist Tivet?"

"Most assuredly: not content with demonic associations, the accused also desired victory for our bitter enemies!"

"I thank you, Sir Seneschal. . . ."

Tiadann returned to his seat and the archimandrite continued his interrogation.

"A final point remains to be cleared up. Some people claim that you have resurrected the dead. What do you say to this, Alterdo?"

"These statements are somewhat exaggerated. All I did was treat a few sick people—to tell the truth they were in very bad shape—but I have no power to rekindle life."

"Call forth the woman of Riemm!" ordered the president.

A gentlewoman in a long purple velvet robe came before the court and took the oath.

"Tell us exactly what happened, gentle lady."

"Gentlemen, what follows is an exact account of events. My eldest son, stricken by a malignant fever, had been given up for dead by all the doctors. The drugs prescribed by the apothecaries only worsened his state. At my wit's end, and with no sin in mind, I heeded the advice of several of my friends who spoke to me in the highest terms of the miracles performed by Alterdo Zanzini. Going to see him, I told him of my despair, and he agreed to come with me for the sum of fifty gold pistoles.

"When we entered my poor child's room, the maid was sitting by his bedside in tears. My son, pale as a sheet, showed not the slightest sign of life. The doctor went up to him and after a brief examination forced a drug down his throat. He had to pry apart his teeth with the handle of a spoon. That done, the magician told me to give my son this product three times a day, and I did as he said. . . ."

"Is there any of this philter left?"

"Alas, sir, no."

"Too bad. But continue."

"Well, at midday my son's complexion suddenly became all pink and he opened his eyes. The next morning he was completely cured."

"We thank you for this crushing testimony, gentle lady. Does anyone care to put a question to this poor mother so sorely abused by a sorcerer?"

Nobody gave any sign, and the lady withdrew. The president of the tribunal then solemnly rose and said: "We are now sufficiently enlightened to determine our sentence. The tribunal will retire to deliberate."

Alterdo showed no sign of emotion. Turning toward Tiadann, he studied him awhile with a sarcastic smile. Then he quietly awaited the return of the venerable servants of the Church. Apparently they had had no trouble coming to agreement, for they quickly returned and resumed their places. Then the archimandrite proclaimed in a solemn voice:

"Our lords the judges, very reverend members of this tribunal, presided over by the archimandrite and endowed with full powers by Our Venerated Sovereign Sranz VII, may God grant him a long and happy life, decree as follows. The accused, Alterdo Zanzini, convicted of being a sorcerer, soothsayer, necromancer, invoker of evil spirits, given to sacrilege, blasphemy, warmongering, and sedition, engendered in his mother's womb by a demon incubus, allied to the Devil by a secret pact, given to making and using magic philters, casting spells, charms, and enchantments, abominable for numerous sins, will for all these crimes be canonically and legally punished. The pernicious contagion must be kept from spreading among the faithful adherents of our religion. Since the facts testified to are clear, we declare that Alterdo Zanzini must be cast out as a gangrenous member of the community of Lonks and turned over to the secular arm. He will immediately be given into the hands of the executioner to be burned alive at the stake. Repent, unhappy soul. There is still time to repent your sins and save yourself from the flames of hell, for those flames are eternal!"

"Cut the nonsense!" interrupted the condemned man. "Let's get this formality over with as quickly as possible. I've had more than enough of your sinister mumbojumbo!"

Upon these contemptuous words, Iern'an rose and strode firmly toward the door that led to the palace courtyard where the executioner awaited him. The tribunal remained in the audience chamber, since ecclesiastics spilled no blood; the secular authorities carried out their sentences.

A crowd hungry for morbid pleasures had been waiting by the stake for hours, and the guards could hardly clear the way for the condemned man. Idlers and ruffians shouted abuse and taunts at Alterdo, who continued to bear himself with courage: it was as though he in no way feared the terrible fate that awaited him.

His brave demeanor ended by winning the respect of all, and soon a dead silence reigned over the place of torture.

Tiadann, escorted by two halberdiers, had taken his place in the front ranks of those present. Alterdo saw him and kept staring at him fixedly as the executioner bound his hands. Despite himself, the seneschal was upset, and raising his psychic barrier he assured the victim:

"Don't worry, old friend. This disagreeable formality will not last long. Keep tight control on your neurons and you won't feel a thing! Oh, one small detail. The spaceship is just above us. You can't get to it, but the module is right alongside, and in it is everything you asked me for."

"Thanks for your concern!" bantered Alterdo. "You wouldn't care to exchange places with me, would you?"

"My task here is not complete, as you well know. I'll keep you closely informed of events. . . ."

The exchange stopped there, for the executioner, aided by his assistants, was hauling the condemned man onto a pile of fagots and attaching him to a stake driven into the ground. He then placed on Alterdo's head a conical bonnet bearing in large letters the following words: *sorcerer*, *necromancer*, *heretic*. Finally the executioner descended from the pyre and applied a torch to all four corners. Bright flames sprang up immediately, and the wood began to crackle.

A deep murmur ran through the spectators. Women covered their eyes with their hands and began to sob. Soon the flames were licking at the feet of the condemned man, who remained impassive with his eyes fixed on Tiadann; his lips curled in an enigmatic and mocking smile. Soon he was half hidden in smoke. His sumptuous clothes began to shrivel in the flames. The wood crackled and the fire rose high above the stake.

Alterdo continued to remain silent. Nevertheless, when the swirling smoke dissipated for a moment, those watching could see his flesh crackling and swelling, while a nauseating odor spread through the air.

A few women, unable to bear it any longer, fainted. And just then an amazing phenomenon took place. Above the sorcerer's head, a luminous sphere rose into the sky. Its brightness was such that it outshone that of the flames. Exclamations of stupefaction exploded from the crowd.

The shining object floated lazily in the air, while inside, what looked like fireflies seemed to be making curious configurations.

The crowd instinctively drew back. Assuredly, this was the demon's way of appearing and proving that he was all-powerful. He had come to seize the soul that had been consecrated to him from birth.

In spite of themselves, the guards raised their pikes as though in self-defense. Bluish lightning shot off from the metallic points, crackling as the bolts joined in midair. Several of the halberdiers experienced violent shocks and sank to the paving stones in terror. Panic-stricken, the crowd raced off at top speed, frightened lest it be the object of demonic vengeance. The soldiers, rising to their tottering legs, fled after them without further ado.

Only the seneschal remained in the square, imperturbable. He saw the sphere whirl around, slowly gaining altitude as it shot forth lightning that struck the pointed weathervanes, driving the Lonks out of their minds with terror.

Then the thing sped into the sky, quickly becoming smaller and smaller. Soon only a shiny spot remained visible, and finally it too disappeared into the heavy clouds.

A torrential downpour fell on the square, extinguishing the glowing embers and drowning the grayish ashes that were the only remains of the tortured body.

For a long time Tiadann remained immobile, indifferent to the water that flowed down his face and soaked his clothes.

Finally the rain ceased. A few guards timidly reappeared, followed by the executioner and his aides, who took up shovels and loaded the charred remains into wicker baskets which were then to be emptied into the river, as was the custom.

For some inexplicable reason the sorcerer's ashes had remained dry, as though the rain had had no power to dampen them! While they were at work, the executioner's crew came upon a piece of shining metal that the heat had not been able to melt. Its delicate convolutions had remained intact . . . Since nobody was bold enough to touch it, the thing, whatever it was, was shoveled into the baskets containing the ashes.

Just then a psychic message reached Tiadann: "Well, this little ceremony went off easily enough, my dear countryman! At most, all I felt was a slight warmth in my toes. Thanks for the module—I'm very comfortable in it. And so now you're rid of me. Have fun. . . ."

The seneschal made no reply. In spite of himself he was wondering why the professor had kept smiling so slyly. In theory, the old fogey could no longer interfere with him, but something about his attitude had suggested that he was far from beaten. . . . Shaking his head, the seneschal returned to the royal palace.

In the days that followed, tongues wagged mightily in the city. Every spectator told his own version of events, and soon there was talk that a fire-eating dragon had sprung from the sorcerer's body. Despite ecclesiastical assurances, the population feared that the powerful demon might wreak his wrath on them, and the merchants of amulets reaped a fortune.

But calm was soon restored. The news from the army was excellent: the Lonkian host went from victory to victory. The Duke of Xovia, severely defeated, sent a herald to King Sranz and sued for peace. He was willing to swear loyalty to the king and even to furnish a contingent of troops to be used in the attack upon the island of the Incls.

Following Tiadann's advice, Sranz rejected these peace offers. Ardez and Moruns received orders to capture the duke dead or alive. Fighting was resumed in the mountains bordering Xovia. Then one spring day the news of the valiant duke's death reached Aniar. His body, half devoured by wild animals, had been found near the icy waters of a small mountain lake.

There was an immediate outbreak of general and unrestrained joy. Drunken processions wound through the streets bawling songs in praise of the military prowess of the Lonkian leaders. Liane was by no means forgotten.

She was only a humble country maid
Who guarded her flocks in the green, green
spring
Though sweet and gentle, she was unafraid
And at eighteen she was brought to the king.

Up to the sovereign she goes to curtsey
Sweet lady, jests he, it's really not me
Kind sire, gentle sire, you make my heart ache
But with God's help, I can make no mistake.

Everybody praised the military accomplishments of

the little shepherdess. Ever since she had had the king consecrated, the affairs of the kingdom had flourished. The merchants could resume their activities in peace, and the cloth trade with the North had started up again. Even the peasants finally knew tranquility. Constant warfare had prevented cultivation of the land, for at any moment an armed band might have appeared from nowhere, set fire to the grain crops, pillaged the farms, and led off the cattle and sheep; but now the Lonks no longer had to fear either the Incls or the Xovians.

As soon as the army returned, Ardez was given Xovia as his fief, and he rendered homage to Sranz. From all corners of the land, knights eager to participate in the conquest of the Incl island came to fill the ranks of the royal army.

Tiadann was delighted to be with his friends once more. As for them, they warmly congratulated him on his diligence: a powerful fleet had been assembled on the channel coast. Ships from the North and the South had come to swell the armada, and as a result the size of the Lonkian naval squadrons equaled that of the Incls.

The weather was magnificent, and the Lonks felt they had to take advantage of it to sail across the channel while it was calm; because of this, the host remained in the capital for only two days. Troops and artillery were embarked upon the heavy barges, which began the descent of the Rifen. On the lead boat, Liane's banner waved proudly in the breeze while the military leaders worked out the final details of the invasion.

None of them knew much about maritime affairs, so Liane had expressly asked the king to name the seneschal grand admiral. All the councillors had warmly supported this request, and Tiadann was therefore awarded this new rank. Thus it was he who spoke first.

"All our manpower problems have been resolved, and we have enough ships and barges to transport the army overseas. In addition, I have been able to solve the supply problems: the armada will carry with it a million flasks of wine, five quintals of preserved meat, two thousand quintals of cheese, five thousand quintals of salted fish, four thousand quintals of wheat, and fifty thousand hectoliters of drinking water. The rich Ronande countryside has furnished part of these provisions, and the rest came up the coast from the southern provinces."

"Great balls of fire!" laughed Ardez, "that's more than we need to cross such a narrow stretch of sea. It won't take the fleet more than two days to reach the other side of the channel. . . ."

"Agreed, but we have to allow a fairly large margin. For example, the winds may not be favorable for quite some time. In addition, our adversaries are formidable fighters. In spite of their recent reverses, the campaign may go on for several months, and if they decide to follow a scorched-earth policy, our troops will not be able to live off the land!"

"Very foresighted!" Moruns said approvingly. "But I hope the admiral hasn't forgotten an ample provision of amunition?"

"Nothing to worry about. We'll be carrying with us one hundred field pieces and ten thousand cannonballs. In addition there are portable weapons that an ingenious Douir armorer has made some refinements on. I'm willing to bet that their accuracy will surprise you."

"But we will have to fight the Incl fleet before we

can reach the other shore," Liane broke in. "That fight may well be a murderous one, since the enemy cannon will wreak havoc on our overloaded ships. . . ."

"There too the ingenuity of the Lonkian artisans has come to our aid, gentle Maid! Fifty thousand balls and twenty thousand pounds of powder are destined for the ships' artillery. We also now have a useful mechanism that will make it possible to aim the guns laterally. The Incls will first have to orient their vessels before firing, but we won't."

"Hell's bells!" exclaimed Ardez in admiration. "The things that are invented these days! Those Incls had better watch out. Now I understand why their deserters have reported that the island was in the grip of fear! With all these diabolic machines, we are invincible. . . ."

"But tell me, faithful Tiadann," continued the Maid; "Aren't you afraid that the soldiers of our host may be greatly discomforted by the crossing? As for me, I've never been on a ship before, and I'm very fearful of finding myself surrounded on all sides by water. I've also heard it said that the atmosphere of these ships is pestilential. After a few hours, the hulls are cesspools overflowing with the vomit and excrement of the sailors and passengers."

"I've given some thought to this problem, too. Each ship will carry a number of clay pots that can used to dump pestilential matter. The officers will be issued sticks of incense, and the smoke will sweeten the air as it disinfects it."

"What a valuable man you are!" exclaimed Moruns. "You've obviously thought of everything! But I do have to point out one problem: our barges and hookers may not be able to draw close to the rocky coast. How can we disembark our horses?"

"I've been very careful to choose favorable landing spots on the Incl coast," replied Tiadann, spreading out some scrolls on which the configuration of the shore and the depth of water had been carefully recorded—thanks to photographs taken by his spaceship.

"Marvelous!" breathed Liane, enraptured. "Every bay, every promontory is shown. But how can you be sure of bringing the fleet to these precise points? I'm told that navigation is still a fairly uncertain art."

"Once more I was able to make use of discoveries by our good Lonkian artisans! The rigging of the ships has been modified so that they now have three masts and can be handled more easily. By day we will use magnetic stones from the North; they are cut into bars that always orient themselves toward the place in which they were extracted from the ground. . . ."

Ardez and Moruns, their eyes shining with excitement, were as amused as children as they endlessly turned the boxes in which needles, mounted on pivots, kept swinging back in the same direction.

". . . At night, all we'll have to do is shine a light on them—and besides, the stars will be of help. Any other objections, gentlemen?"

"A man would have to be a knave not to congratulate you," sighed the bastard. "But tell me, Tiadann, how have you learned of all these marvels? I've never before heard tell of them!"

"I keep open house for travelers, magicians, and learned men," the savant answered simply, "and I hear many tales of far-off countries. Sometimes they seem almost incredible. For example, I was recently even told that the form of our Earth was round."

"Another astonishing marvel!" said Ardez in amazement. "According to you, then, if a ship were to keep sailing toward the sunset, it would end up where it started from?"

"So I'm told."

"Good Lord, what a time we live in!" concluded Moruns. "Some day you'll have to take me to the antipodes. Once the Incls are defeated, life will become very monotonous. . . ."

And so the conference came to a close, but as a result, the aureole that surrounded the new admiral increased. Nobody could find terms too extravagant to praise his zeal and his remarkable capacities.

But everything that had gone before was as nothing compared with the moment when the Lonkian leaders sailed out of the estuary and spotted their majestic fleet lying at anchor, each hull outlined against the gold of the setting sun. . . .

Chapter Six

Despite their courage, the Lonks couldn't help feeling somewhat fearful at the idea of having to cross the channel under enemy fire. The majority of them had never been on a ship before, and their experience in land warfare would be of no use to them . . .

The grand admiral was well aware of this state of affairs and decided to get his troops used to the sea as soon as possible. Each contingent had been assigned to specific quarters, and the embarkment began as soon as the host arrived.

The first thing was to load the horses; block and tackle helped to hoist them aboard. Generally speaking, things went well; some of the hawsers broke and dropped the steeds into the water, but only a few of them were drowned.

In addition, some men were hurt when they had their ribs kicked in. As was her wont, Liane cared for them without sparing herself; she bathed their wounds, gave those who were most severely injured food and drink, reassured the more frightened among them, and had them brought to a comfortable house near the port. Such attentions profoundly touched the hearts of these rough men, who would have died for their heroic Maid.

The soldiers and arbalesters were brought on board

in dinghies, and during this operation too there were several accidental dunkings. The knights and equerries went directly from the wharves to the ships. Many of them complained of the narrow quarters assigned them, but since their leaders had no better lodgings, the protests were pointless.

When the entire army had embarked. Tiadann decided to have his fleet perform several exercises so that everybody aboard could find his sea legs. As it happened, the wind was against them at first and they would have to wait for the right moment before they could set out to sea. Gunners and arbalesters therefore underwent their apprenticeship as the vessels moved around in two separate formations a few cable lengths from the shore. The marksmen learned how to run up the ropes and get off a few balls or arrows at enemy ships, should any stray within close enough range, and the bombard crews, especially those of the galliots, learned how to aim their heavy iron tubes. Practice shots were taken at some old wrecks in the harbor.

Initially the results were rather disappointing. The swell interfered with the firing and the gunners had to learn to allow for the movement of the ship: the shot had to go off when the vessel was on the crest of the waves so that the range would be augmented.

Little by little the artillery men familiarized themselves with the difficult art of naval combat, and soon the targets were being smashed to smithereens. The generous prizes offered by the admiral helped stimulate enthusiasm, and at the end of ten days of exercises, each man knew what he had to do during the battle.

The pilots maneuvered skillfully, the sailors rapidly supplied the pieces with powder and ball. Nor were the men in the rigging forgotten: they received baskets of arrows and balls for the lightweight arms. The new firing system was put to the test, and even a heavy downpour failed to silence the weapons equipped with flintlocks.

Liane's equerry also proved himself invaluable: his gaiety and humor helped the soldiers forget the pitch and roll of the ships. One of his songs even became famous, and everybody shouted it in chorus whenever seasickness threatened:

The Incl archer is off to the fray
Leaving his keys with the good curé
Having made his will as an Incl should
He entrusted his wife to old Vicar Good
Re, re to the curé

The Incl archer was well equipped
His lance was a twisted roasting spit
He girded on a spoon for a sword
And for helmet only a pot could afford
Re, re to the curé

The Incl archer had a magnificent bow
With which death and destruction to sow
Made of rotten wood and cord that was weathered
It had arrows of paper that were painted and feathered
Re, re to the curé

Thanks to the strenuous training program, the soldiers and sailors had little leisure in which to become bored. But as time went on, the summer heat began to make all these hardy fellows—crammed into badly ventilated hulls—uncomfortable.

Every day the grand admiral consulted his spaceship and drew up a meteorological map based on aerial photographs, but the wind kept blowing landward. . . .

On their island, the Incls were beginning to regain hope: their fleet was being reinforced every day and freely cruised the channel. Contingents coming from far-off countries of the North swelled the army massed not far from the coast near places favorable to a landing.

Even their artillery was beginning to recover its strength; the forges glowed day and night. Cannon were being cast and ammunition amassed. Not a single toad was left on the island, every one having been captured to renew the supplies of incapacitants compounded according to new formulae which it was hoped would surprise the invaders.

Tiadann had not overlooked chemical arms either: he had improved Liane's primitive antidepressants and accumulated a large number of telecommanded spheres in his spaceship.

None of this kept the Lonks from grumbling. They had counted on a fast campaign and here they were piled into ships, waiting for a fair wind. . . . There were already defections; barks disappeared, a few ships slipping away every night never to be seen again.

Finally the grand admiral's patience and efforts were rewarded. The instruments aboard his spaceship informed him that an anticyclone was forming over the continent: the winds along the coast were finally going to blow toward the island of the Incls. To the great amazement of Moruns and Ardez, since the breeze was at present still unfavorable, Tiadann began getting everybody ready.

One night the stars became veiled, and clouds blanketed the skies. A small squall soaked the ships and finally cooled things off a bit, bringing relief to all. Then the sea became wrinkled with small waves: in the morning, the main mast of the admiral's ship finally carried the signal for getting under way. Immediately, the armada majestically moved out to sea. The training during those long days of waiting was bearing fruit. The warships, which were fastest, sailed on ahead and covered the right wing, while the barges and hookers took the shortest way across the channel. The grand admiral was on his way to meet the enemy.

Aerial photographs taken during the preceding days of good weather had made it possible for Tiadann to pinpoint the location of the enemy ships which were still cruising the coasts to the north of the Lonkian ships.

Now the wind was blowing directly toward the Incls, who had to tack about to keep themselves from being carried outside the channel. Actually, the clouds the Incls so cursed were protecting them from the prying eyes of the spaceship, which was floating over their heads. Tiadann had to make use of his considerably less accurate infrared apparatus.

As for the Incls, the thick weather made them strain their eyes in an effort to catch sight of the Lonkian ships.

On board the invasion fleet, the captains assembled their crews in order to read them the grand admiral's battle orders:

> Our ships must take maximum advantage of their maneuverability to fight without getting close up: our superiority in artillery will make it possible to

wreak havoc with the enemy vessels. In case certain ships lose contact during the battle, their magnetic needles and the navigators' innate sense of direction should permit them to reassemble at the mouth of the river leading to Linr.

The hookers and barges will disembark their troops south of the river mouth. The objective of these troops the first day will be to establish a solid beachhead whose right wing will be protected by the river.

Every Incl on the island now knows that the Lonkian fleet is cutting across the channel under a favorable wind. Don't count on the effect of surprise. Initially, there will be little enemy action, as the greater part of their forces are massed farther north. However, the days following the landing will be decisive.

Men of Lonk, you have demonstrated your valor in booting the enemy out of your country. This time you will be fighting on Incl soil. The enemy in turn will learn of the misfortunes of war. I am certain that we will be victorious and that each man will do his duty!

A few feeble cheers were heard at the end of this harangue: The nausea that twisted the guts of these landlubbers shaken by the choppy sea did not allow for the expression of much more enthusiasm than that.

Meanwhile Tiadann had the fleet tack about until the cargo ships could catch up with the greater part of the armada. His orders were transmitted by a signal code based on flags.

The night passed without incident. In the early morning the armada was no longer very far from the Incl fleet, which was widely dispersed, since its not very maneuverable vessels had trouble tacking before the wind. The better captains had managed not to be carried too far; the others stayed behind.

A compact formation had been maintained by the Lonks, however. In the center were the ships under the grand admiral's direct command; slightly forward of these were the two wings commanded respectively by Moruns on the port side and Ardez on the starboard.

The Maid was on the flagship. She, alas, hadn't found her sea legs and suffered greatly from the bad weather. Pale as a sheet, she lay holed up in the captain's cabin on the poopdeck.

Tiadann, leaning into the wind, kept close to the helmsman, discreetly consulting his spaceship so as to check on the enemy position. The Incls, however, remained uncertain of what was going on, for the morning fog made any visual spotting impossible.

When the grand admiral had ascertained that the two forces were close, he had a scarlet flag hoisted on the main mast of his vessel. The signal was immediately repeated from ship to ship. Rushing to their cannon, the gun crews prepared the linstocks; meanwhile the harquebusiers climbed into the rigging and readied their weapons for possible close combat.

As the trumpets resounded, hookers and barges moved off toward the south, leaving a free field for the battleships. Tiadann had preferred getting them out of danger to keeping them in the center of his formation, where there might have been some ill-timed collisions when the heavy cargo ships turned slowly during the course of the battle.

The Incls' long experience in navigation kept them from being taken totally by surprise. They had moved many light and maneuverable ships into a fanlike formation of luggers, flyboats, and small fishing vessels whose captains knew every inch of the channel, and it was these ships that spotted the Lonkian fleet when she sailed out of the morning mist; running before the wind, they sped off to give the alarm.

The imminence of the clash had like a miracle cured even those who were most seasick, and all—sailors and landlubbers alike—peered into the grayish horizon in order to have the honor of being the first to spot the enemy fleet.

In spite of the warning of the scouts, the Incl ships barely had time to regroup. Some withdrew toward where the mass of the fleet was assembled, but as they did so, their unarmed sterns were subjected to fire from Tiadann's vessels.

Everything went off as though in a parade-ground exercise. The Lonks, in a tight formation, caught up with the fleeing enemy one by one. The gunners, sighting and aiming with cold efficiency, massacred the unfortunates who were involuntarily guiding them toward their compatriots. In this phase of the battle the galliots proved extremely valuable. Their turret-mounted bombards made it possible to take precise aim on the enemy masts, which when hit fell rumbling onto the decks, leaving the ships helpless under heavy Lonkian fire. At almost no time did the assailants have to confront formations. With the wind behind it, Tiadann's more maneuverable armada bore down on the Incl ships and put one after another out of action.

The admiral commanding the defense forces reacted quickly, ordering his captains to disperse toward the port and starboard and then to bear down on the flanks of the invading fleet.

It was the turn of Moruns and Ardez to distinguish

themselves. Neither man was a sailor, but the mobility of their ships made it possible for them to be directed like squadrons of cavalry. The skill of the artillery did the rest so well that the Incls suffered another defeat. The leeward sea was covered with smoking unmasted wrecks which were the prey of the Lonkian rear guard.

In desperation, the Incl admiral tried another tactic. Emerald pennants went up his masts and gave the signal to grapple to. Demonstrating the stubbornness of their race, the surviving captains scrupulously did as they were commanded, and pointed their vessels toward the flanks of the Lonkian armada.

Once again the superiority of the artillery developed by Tiadann was crushing. His adversaries, whose hulls careened about, could hardly get off a shot. They therefore had to once more submit to a hail of cannon fire, and many of them were set ablaze. The noxious fumes of powder, sulfur, and tar suffocated the crews, who jumped overboard to escape the inferno.

Despite all this, a few Incl ships managed to come within harquebus range. At this point, the Lonks began to pepper them with both the bombards and the lightweight arms. The decks were flowing with blood and littered with torn limbs and bits of flesh. Only a few of these valiant fighters managed to toss grapples onto the ships commanded by Ardez and Moruns. Their numbers were so small that the Lonks had no trouble fighting off their adversaries. Passing to the offensive, they even managed to capture several Incl vessels.

Just then the clouds dispersed and the sun lit up the battleground. As far as the eye could see, there was nothing but broken hulls and masts trailing in the water, mutilated bodies and staved-in ships bouncing up and down on the waves. The Incl admiral could no longer delude himself: the engagement had ended in a disaster. He had only some twenty ships left intact, a laughable number with which to oppose a landing.

A clear-minded man, this valiant sailor therefore sent some fast tenders toward the coast to warn Rog Bacdir that the Lonks were going to land unopposed.

While the butchers and executioners, acting as surgeons, axed off splintered limbs, their aides cauterized the stumps with hot irons.

Then the Incl admiral made one final attempt to save the rest of his fleet. His captains knew by heart the shoals, reefs, and treacherous sandbanks along the coast; he therefore gave orders for his ships to shift direction once more, and those nearest the island scudded on a port tack toward the gray line outlining the horizon. The others, less lucky, fled before their adversaries with the wind in their sails.

As for Tiadann, he had had enough. Putting his second in command in charge, he signaled Ardez and Moruns to follow him in order to protect the cargo ships that should now have been very close to the landing beaches. The estuary had to be penetrated if reinforcements were to be prevented from reaching the Incl coastal defenses.

For a time the armada whipped along, wind on the quarter, passing incredible heaps of debris, remains of the battle, hogsheads, baskets and chicken coops mingled with bodies and spars. Liane, who had come out for air, couldn't bear the sight, and once again sought shelter in the captain's quarters.

Meanwhile, joy reigned on board. Wine barrels were tapped and emptied in the twinkling of an eye and the sailors devoured the not very appealing skilligalee that was dished out to them; their appetites were suddenly so ferocious that they didn't leave so much as a drop.

As Tiadann had foreseen, the weather improved, but the wind remained brisk and joyfully propelled the ships toward the Incl shores.

The grand admiral signaled Moruns and Ardez to disembark their troops while he himself tacked about in the estuary to the right of the beaches. By evening the Lonkian fleet had joined up with the barges and hookers floating at anchor a few cable lengths from the coast.

Since nobody and nothing now threatened them, Tiadann ordered his men to take a well-earned rest. The landing would take place in the morning right after dawn, when the tide was in. The meteorological bulletins from the spaceship forcast splendid weather, and he expected the operation to proceed without much difficulty. Once this was arranged, the grand admiral went off to rejoin the Maid and dine in her company.

The flagship had received little damage, but Tiadann's splendid uniform had nevertheless been torn in places by splintering wood, and he was spotted with blood from a man who had been hit in the yards above the helm. In the heat of action he had paid no attention to it. But when Liane saw him, she was horrified.

"May the Archangel Lignel pardon me!" she moaned. "Have you been wounded, Tiadann?"

"No, I don't think so. . . ."

"Let me make sure," said the Maid, carefully examining the admiral's arms and chest.

As she did so, she cleaned up the bloodspots with a cloth.

"No, honestly, I haven't been wounded anywhere."

"Then what's this?" asked Liane, pointing to a long gash in her friend's forearm. "That's a deep cut, and it should be bandaged. I can't understand why it isn't bleeding. . . ."

Uneasy, Tiadann tried to distract the young girl. Might she not begin to suspect his extraterrestrial origin?

"Let it be! It's nothing, compared to the terrible wounds of all those other poor wretches. There's no point in bothering about it!"

"Don't be foolish! We have great need of you right now. This wound has to be bathed and disinfected . . ."

And so saying, the girl grabbed a bottle of brandy and uncorked it.

"Careful now, it's going to burn," she warned as she spilled a little of the liquid over the cut.

The admiral felt nothing. Like his friend Alterdo, he could disconnect his neurons whenever he wished, but still he thought it might be best to register some protest.

"Ouch! You're hurting me!"

"Come, don't be such a baby. Now I'll bind up your arm and in a day or two you won't be able to see a trace. . . ."

Upon which, she tore off a few strips of cloth and with them bandaged the wounded arm.

Meanwhile Tiadann asked: "And what about you? How did you manage during the ups and downs of the battle?"

"Oh, I thought I was going to give up the ghost! I felt sick to my stomach almost all the time! The sight of these horrors is more than I can bear: war is really a scourge! At one point the sea was covered with mutilated bodies. I was overcome with self-disgust—and this is only the beginning! Now we have to fight on land! My God! when will men stop slaughtering one another?"

She had finished her bandaging, and Tiadann sat down at the table while she brought him a flask of wine, some bread, and a piece of salted meat.

"Ah, that's exactly how I feel!" sighed her guest as he cut himself a large slice of bread. "Listen, Liane, I think that our true mission has only begun. . . ."

"What do you mean?" she said, throwing him a penetrating glance. "Could you too be guided by celestial visions?"

"Perhaps . . . In my dreams I often see winged creatures who talk to me about you. Could they be angels?"

"No doubt about it!" assured the Maid, clasping her hands together. "Tell me quickly! What do they say to you?"

"Well, my dreams are almost always the same. They urge me to help you in your task so that the Duke of Fnar can be freed and the Incls once and for all prevented from doing any harm. Next . . ."

He hesitated a moment.

"Speak! I'm burning to know if you have received the same instructions I have."

". . . Next, the winged creatures sigh and weep in pity over the sadness of the human condition. That's why I say that our task has only begun. They want war to disappear from Noldaz forever!"

"That's exactly it!" approved Liane ecstatically. "The Archangel Lignel says the same kind of thing to me."

"All the nations must be united, they say. And to do that we will have to impose the same language on every kingdom of Noldaz. Once the island of the

Incls is conquered, the Lonks will establish schools in which a universal language will be taught. The same will be true in Xovia and in all the other countries, even those beyond the seas. . . ."

"That's strange," remarked the Maid. "My voices haven't said anything to me about that. Are there peoples we know nothing about?"

"Yes indeed! I've received great revelations about that. Noldaz is a sphere, and man can therefore journey completely around it in a ship. Such circumnavigation will make it possible to establish contact with backward peoples. They too will have to acknowledge the true religion and learn the universal language."

"By all the saints, I'm amazed! We will have to lead a veritable crusade across the vast world . . . fight without cease. . . . The infidels occupy powerful kingdoms to the south, beyond the seas. How can we accomplish so vast a task?"

"All the peoples on this continent will help us! We will share the burden. Ardez will fight in the South, Moruns in the North, and you and I will lead an armada to the West, to an immense continent that we will bring to civilization!"

"I can see that you are animated by an unshakable faith, Tiadann! In truth, a hard task has been assigned us, but we will not disappoint our celestial guides, and since such is the price of definitive peace, we will conquer the world! But tell me, do you think our king will be willing to give us the necessary men, money, and supplies? I've already had trouble enough convincing him to chase the Incls from the kingdom. . . ."

"Fear nothing, Liane," said the grand admiral reassuringly, as he affectionately placed his hand on the young girl's shoulder. "Heaven has given me powerful means of persuasion. I will know how to convince him of his duty."

"Ah, my friend, what would happen to me without you? From our very first meeting I felt myself powerfully attracted to you. I was aware of enormous sympathy for you without knowing why. I now know that henceforth I am no longer alone. Heaven has granted me a lieutenant who will sustain my courage. Nevertheless, the immensity of this mission terrifies me. How many of those who will have to fight for our Holy Cause will perish along the way?"

"Assuredly, there will be hell on earth. But remember that those who are struck down will attain to Heaven because they will have obeyed the celestial commands. We will be aided in our task by our visions. Even before this battle, they had already given me orders to talk to the Lonkian artisans and show them how to improve our fleet and our artillery. This made it possible for us to be victorious with a minimum of losses. In my dreams, other visions have encouraged me to develop arms comparable to those of the Incls. Beyond the seas, there are substances even more powerful than their toad venom. Thanks to these our armies will be able to plunge our adversaries into a deep sleep. And once that's done, what could be easier than to disarm them? In this way our conquests will cause hardly any deaths at all. For that very reason, it is my intention to sail off with the armada as soon as the Incls are beaten, so we can acquire these marvelous substances and give them to the armies that will fight for us on this continent."

"Your words are so captivating that I never get tired of listening to you. Oh, yes! Be quick. Go in search of these magic drugs that will bring an end to all this slaughter. . . ."

"Alas, we must first finish with these accursed Incls," sighed Tiadann hypocritically. "Tomorrow will be a trying day, but the day after will be even more so."

"Why is that?"

"The disembarkment of our troops will probably be met with little opposition. On the other hand, as soon as our contingents are on the land, the Incl army will try to cross the river and attack them. There will then be many deaths and innumerable wounded. . . ."

"It is the price we have to pay to bring a durable peace to this poor world which is torn apart by so many opposing factions. Remember that Noldaz will become a Paradise when all the united peoples speak the same language. There will be an end to the curse that struck them when God scattered them and imposed the cruel ordeal of war among humans of the same flesh but different cultures and languages! But I take my oath on it: beginning tomorrow, I will organize a corps of devoted people who will pass through the battlefield to search out and care for all the wounded, without regard for country. . . ."

"That's a good and wise decision. For my part I will try to furnish carts and skiffs so that the wounded can be brought on board our ships. That way I can treat them with simple but helpful drugs. . . ."

"I recognize your goodness in that, Tiadann! Thus we will have tried to help our fellow creatures to the extent that we can. . . . But here I am drinking in your words like some poor mad creature, and you've long since finished your meal. You must be dying for sleep! An arduous day awaits you tomorrow. Go now, it's time to get some rest."

"To tell the truth, you're right," agreed Tiadann, yawning. "The night is already far gone. We've nothing to fear from the Incl fleet. Even as we have been talking, my second in command has chased them far from here. Good night, Liane, I'm going to bed. . . ."

"May heaven protect you and give you tranquil sleep," said the Maid with a tender smile. "Tomorrow I will be at the side of our valiant soldiers. I am braver on land than I am on the sea!"

As Tiadann left to return to the adjacent cabin he stepped over the body of Liane's equerry, who like a faithful hound was sleeping outstretched before her door. Seating himself on the edge of his mat, he turned off the psycho-inductor that had made it possible for him to convince the Maid so easily. This done, he established communication with his spaceship. The computer on board confirmed its preceding meteorological bulletin: there would be fine weather and sunshine all day. The wind would remain gentle and blow from the east.

Reassured, Tiadann stretched out on his bed and continued to think. No sign of Alterdo; he must be spending his time playing the psychic tapes on the module that had been placed at his disposal. One thing was certain: he had made no attempt to penetrate the energy barrier protecting the spaceship. And since the light vessel in which he was lodged had no radio equipment, there was no need to fear the intervention of Galactic Inspectors in the near future.

Fortune continued to smile upon the vast enterprise launched by the rebel. He was sure that as his experiment proceeded, his calls on the resources of the spaceship would involve more and more risks.

The conquest of the planet would call for the massive use of incapacitants, and in the long run this would arouse the suspicions of the inspectors. But by the time that happened, it would be too late to turn back. Given a *fait accompli*, the Galactic Council could only confirm the measures that had been taken.

The grand admiral closed his eyes and disconnected his senses, but not before he had as usual turned on the warning mechanism that protected him. He immediately fell into a deep sleep.

Chapter Seven

At dawn the next day, the disembarkment began. The shallops forming the first wave surged out of the light mist and soon struck against the sandy beach; arbalesters, armed with flintlock weapons that they held over their heads, rushed forward.

They crossed the beach without running into any more opposition than sporadic fire from coastal patrols hidden in the underbrush. Racing ahead, the Lonks took up positions behind the cliffs overlooking the little bay.

In the mist they could see the multicolor sails of the barges and hookers approaching in turn, their pennants and flags flapping in the wind. They ran aground a short way from land and began to unload their knights and horses.

Soon a veritable motley colony of ants swarmed over the beach. The horses sniffed the nearby fresh country odors and began to whinny, the captains barked orders at their troops, the flags and banners snapped in the breeze.

Liane, Ardez, and Moruns were among the first to set foot on the island, and they immediately separated to head their respective detachments.

The Maid's objective was a small port situated south of the landing beaches: its occupation would facilitate the unloading of the heavy bombards, so it was therefore necessary to capture it with all possible speed. While Ardez and Moruns plunged inland, Liane, upright on her white palfrey, her banner in her hand, moved at the head of a handpicked group, following a path that wound toward the humble fishermen's dwellings.

The Incls had left only a small garrison there, and so the take-over operation was carried out without difficulty. One after another the cottages were taken, and soon the first Lonkian ships were able to unload heavy artillery. The curses of sailors hauling on pulley blocks replaced the cries of the combatants.

While this was going on, the contingents continued to pour ashore in perfect order. Rog Bacdir had apparently decided against fighting on the seacoast. He had assembled his units inland and planned a decisive counterattack that would drive the invaders back into the sea.

Thanks to his spaceship, Grand Admiral Tiadann was perfectly aware of his adversary's intention; he had a great number of his warships sail up the estuary in order to cut the bridges upriver so that the Incl army would arrive too late to launch a counteroffensive.

But the first thing the Lonks had to do was neutralize the fort commanding the estuary. The galliots therefore boldly advanced toward the shore under the imprecise fire of the enemy artillery. When they were within range, their bombards opened up, first with cannonballs to overturn the earthworks that protected the fort, and then with case shots that cut down the gunners.

The fighting was hard; the enemy gunners had perfectly pre-established their ranges and angles of fire, and as a result, direct hits were scored on several Lonkian vessels.

A few exploded and caught fire; drifting seaward with the current, they spread disorder among the ships waiting at the mouth of the river. Others sank, becoming dangerous wrecks blocking the arrival of reinforcements.

In addition, cannonballs proved ineffective against the thick earthen breastworks and merely lodged themselves without doing much damage. As for the case shots, they simply passed harmlessly over the bundles of brushwood protecting the gunners.

At Zero hour plus three the Lonkian squadron had still not managed to penetrate the fairway. Furious, Tiadann had all his ships draw close and begin a systematic pounding of the accursed fortifications. This time the stubbornness of the defenders was no match for the density of the fire. A few rounds of Greek fire set the neighboring brush aflame and blinded the Incl gunners. Suddenly the galliots could get closer, and furious raking fire finally cut down the defenses and reduced the effectiveness of the protective cover. Case shots liquidated the last survivors; four hours after the beginning of the engagement the Lonkian fleet was finally able to sail up the river.

But the difficulties were far from over.

True, the wind was blowing inland, but it was not very strong, and the ebbtide was beginning to fight against the push of the sails.

Very soon the big ships dropped astern and had to make their way back to the estuary entrance. Only the shallops and barges could forge ahead. A few galleys began hauling those galliots whose artillery was indispensable, but it was midday before they reached the Incl bridges of ships.

Bacdir had had enough time to move three-fourths of his army across the river. His troops were now massing to attack the port and the beaches controlled by the invaders.

In spite of all the information the spaceship had supplied him with, the grand admiral could not keep his adversaries from mounting a counteroffensive after the first day. . . .

And since trouble always comes in pairs, Tiadann received some alarming news: profiting from the ebbing tide, the Incls, experts in all maritime matters, were setting adrift on the river a swarm of small skiffs that had been transformed into fireships!

The Lonkian galliots scarcely had time to get off a hundred rounds against the Incl ammunition convoys proceeding along the riverbanks before they had to retreat in haste. Begun in order, this movement soon turned into a headlong flight, because the fireships were quickly gaining on the Lonkian vessels. Soon a dozen were in flames, and sharpshooters hidden behind the embankments opened a hellish fire on the fleeing ships. . . .

The operation meant to keep Bacdir from transferring troops from one riverbank to the other was ending in a total defeat! As for Tiadann, who had remained at the river mouth with the greater part of his fleet, he was in serious trouble: a clump of Incl barks that had also been transformed into fireships were whipping toward him with the wind in their sails.

To flee the danger, Tiadann gave orders for anchor cables to be cut. Alas, the ships made no headway and were quickly caught up with; only the precision firing of the Lonkian artillery prevented a disaster.

Limping along, as the Lonkian fleet fled south it

soon spread disorder among the cargo ships still discharging troops onto the beaches. Luckily for Tiadann, the Incls had not been able to amass enough fireships, and toward midday the naval counterattack necessarily came to a halt. Disheartened, the grand admiral ordered his armada to tack about in front of the estuary until it could sail upriver on the next tide.

And what was happening on land during this time? The operations led by Ardez and Moruns were proceeding without major difficulties as one after another the barges came to disgorge their passengers on land and sail out again.

In the neighboring port, Liane was directing the unloading of the artillery, and the disembarkation was proceeding smoothly.

Toward five in the afternoon so much had been unloaded that the roads leading inland were overcrowded and the rate at which new ships arrived had to be reduced.

The Lonkian leaders decided to move further inland and get ready to meet Rog Bacdir's expected attack.

A messenger was dispatched to Liane, who came to join Ardez and Moruns on a small hill from which much of the coastal plain could be seen. The view from where they stood was splendid. The green countryside speckled with golden flowers stretched as far as the eye could see; here and there, light clouds of dust indicated the roads along which the two armies were moving. And in the rear, the bluish sea was dotted with hundreds of tiny specks: toylike ships gracefully riding the waves. Toward the north a thick cloud masked the horizon where several vessels continued to burn.

But the Lonkian notables were not there to admire

the countryside; in his usual outspoken way, Liane's equerry said exactly what they were all thinking:

"Damn, what a pity to be slaughtering one another on a beautiful day like this! We'd all be better off seated at some table with a good bottle in front of us!"

"True enough, my good Renouard! However, we mustn't forget our task: we have to beat the Incls in order to free the brave Duke of Fnar. . . ." Liane reminded him.

"Until now we've had nothing to complain about," noted Moruns. "Our army disembarked almost without losses, and we're massed in good order on a battlefield of our own choice. God be praised! Tiadann's information has turned out to be remarkably accurate. . . ."

"It's true that he conducted this operation with extraordinary brilliance," Ardez joined in. "I'd love to have him here with us now! Do you think that Rog Bacdir will attack before nightfall?"

"That's hard to say," sighed Liane. "I think I can make out the enemy positions, but I can't be sure if they're in battle formation."

"I can tell you," chuckled Renouard, cupping his hands to his eyes. "There are three big contingents in front of us. The artillery is in the center because I can make out the smoke of their linstocks. It looks to me as if the cavalry is getting ready to attack our left wing."

The sharpsightedness of the equerry was legendary in the army, and the Lonkian leaders believed what he said. Moruns and Liane hurried off to rejoin their front ranks, while Ardez remained on the hill with messengers mounted on swift steeds. From where he was he had an overall view and could give the alarm if necessary.

The information furnished by Renouard was exact: Rog Bacdir wanted to push the Lonks into the river and onto the beaches by a massive attack with his heavy cavalry.

Without waiting any longer, Ardez therefore gave orders for the Lonkian bombards to start firing cannonballs on the left wing. Moruns had the culverins loaded with case shot, and he and his men prepared to stand firm against the assault.

Liane was in charge of the forces positioned along the river; they were to be the pivot around which the Lonkian army would turn to beat the enemy back toward the river.

All in all, the front on which the troops were going to clash was rather small. On the left, hills bordered the narrow plain alongside the river. Fairly deep slopes made a cavalry attack impossible. The decisive fighting would thus take place in a frontal battle, and fire density would play a considerable role. Nevertheless, the Royal Guard massed in a square in the center of the Incl position could not be ignored. These handpicked giants were expert in swinging battle axes that they held in both hands. With one blow they were capable of splitting an armored knight from head to toe despite his helmet and coat of mail. . . .

The battle began, as was customary, with heavy fire from the crossbowmen and the men carrying harquebuses. The long Incl arrows wreaked havoc in the Lonkian ranks. More than one equerry slumped to the ground, his cuirass pierced through. Next, arrows loaded with incapacitants rained down on the infantry ranks under Moruns' command.

Liane's antidotes did their work so well that nobody

was put out of commission by the volatile venom. Acting on orders received previously, however, the Lonks began to stagger about and collapse, so Rog Bacdir decided that the moment had come to launch his heavy cavalry.

With a thunderous roar, the Incl knights began urging their hardy steel-clad horses onward; hooves hammered against the ground. Banners flapping in the breeze, the flower of King Dronz's nobility rode forward with a shout, their lances pointed toward the quickly retreating footsoldiers. They were soon sorry! The hotheaded nobles learned to their regret that the Lonkian harquebusiers had ceased to be objects of scorn.

Formerly they would make sport of them, proclaiming that the Lonks themselves were terrified of taking aim with these awkward, stumpy, and heavy petards. The scoffers even went so far as to say that their adversaries were more afraid of their own arms than of the enemy's, since one out of every four times their weapons would explode in their hands. . . .

During the battles in Xovia, Liane's harquebusiers had made great progress, adopting a firing technique of fearful efficacity known as "caracoling." After having fired, the front rank would execute a half turn and move off to the side, taking up positions in the rear while they reloaded their arms. The next ranks would then step up and take aim. As a result almost continuous fire power was obtained. In addition, the weapons, modified according to Tiadann's instructions, could be relied on for safety and accuracy. This devilish "caracole" was fatal to many a gallant Incl knight.

The Lonkian left wing, suddenly seeming to regain its vigor, rained a storm of projectiles down on the cavalry dashing toward it. Steeds in the first echelons toppled to the ground. Since those who followed had no time to swing around them, the battlefield was soon sown with unhorsed knights and disemboweled horses whose hooves were tangled in their own entrails.

At this point the Lonkian arbalesters suddenly stopped firing and threw themselves flat on the ground, thereby unmasking the culverins loaded with case shot.

In a few moments, the elite of Incl knighthood was decimated. The attack meant to break the front on the left wing of the disembarked troops had failed completely. . . .

Seizing the opportunity, Moruns loosed his own cavalry. The air suddenly resounded with the blasts of thousands of trumpets. Unstoppable squadrons identified by multicolored pennants surged toward the center of the Incl positions in an avalanche of steel, leaving on their left the debris of the enemy cavalry. Behind them followed the infantry in serried ranks.

Needless to say, the enemy artillery took advantage of this favorable moment to make their guns boom! Cannonballs ripped through the air. Unfortunately, the fire precision left much to be desired. A few knights were brought down like playing cards by this raking fire, but the greater number dashed against the heart of the Incl army like some monstrous wave.

Once there they had to face the battle axes of the Royal Guard, and that was certainly no picnic.

The knights in the first ranks were literally hacked in two, forming a metal barrier which the assault wave avoided by splitting and moving off to either side of their formidable adversaries.

Luckily, the footsoldiers were following, and with them the Lonkian harquebusiers, who once again started up their "caracole" fire, massacring every last one of these expert but unfortunate axmen. This done, the surviving knights were able to return to cleaving the Incl infantry, which was swarming toward the river.

In the center and on the left wing the battle seemed won by the invader. On the right wing, however, Liane had not achieved similarly spectacular results.

Marshy riverbanks made the wholesale use of cavalry impossible, and the encounter was therefore being decided by archers and infantrymen. Marksmen on both sides fired at will for a long time, while soldiers crouching behind the hedges tried to keep out of sight. Liane's equerry had a great deal of trouble restraining the Maid, who, unable to bear this spectacle, wanted to charge without further ado.

Soon ammunition began to run out, and hand-to-hand fighting started. The Lonks, thronged around the white palfrey of their heroine, accomplished miracles, but the Incls did not retreat by so much as a step. Axes whirled, lances rained down ceaselessly. The living trampled over the bodies of the dead and wounded.

Twice Liane's horse went down under her, and if it had not been for the wondrous valor shown by Renouard, the Maid would have been captured.

Grim and undaunted, the warriors went on slaughtering one another pitilessly. Thousands of bodies covered the riverbanks; innumerable corpses floated on the water and were carried toward the sea by the ebbing tide.

In despair, the Maid had seen Tiadann's vessels beat a retreat before the fireships. There was no news from the left wing and she began to fear a defeat.

The day wore on and the sun was already low on

the smoky horizon when the first of those fugitives from the Incl right wing came to sow confusion among the serried ranks of their compatriots. Moruns' troops followed hard behind them.

Surveying the scene from his hilltop command post, Ardez decided that the time had come to attempt a general encirclement.

A courier mounted on a swift thoroughbred brought orders to the Lonkian knights to follow up the offensive toward the river by attacking the enemy rear. Moruns didn't hesitate a moment. His squadrons first swarmed over the Incl artillery, slaughtering the gunners. Rog Bacdir, who was nearby, barely had time to escape to the hills with the surviving Incl knights. The Lonks didn't give chase but continued moving toward the river.

During this time, the grand admiral was far away, near the landing beaches. Furious at his inability to help his friends, he was awaiting the tide so that he could sail up the river and bring the fire of his artillery to the aid of Liane's troops.

Meanwhile, however, he was by no means inactive. Thanks to his spaceship, he had been able to follow the ebb and flow of the battle. The successes achieved by Moruns had gladdened his heart, but the hard fight faced by Liane made him apprehensive. Without the Maid, he would never be able to unite the energies of the Lonkian forces and bring off the task he had set himself.

Until then, the clash between the two armies had gone off in a perfectly classic manner, and no Imperial inspector could have suspected the aid he had given these technologically unsophisticated people.

Now the Incl host was caught in an immense pocket. Its brave soldiers continued to fight valiantly, and they were obviously awaiting nightfall to attempt a river crossing with the help of the innumerable barks amassed upstream—barks that the unexpected fireboat attack had kept the Lonkian fleet from destroying.

A portion of the encircled Incls would of course be slaughtered on the field, but the contingents that managed to escape could march off to swell the defenses of their capital. If this happened, the final victory would be delayed. The battle-seasoned troops that Tiadann desperately needed to undertake new operations on the continent would be in short supply. He therefore had no choice but to intervene. . . .

His supply of incapacitants made it possible for him to sow disorder among the encircled Incl troops, depriving them of courage and energy. Leaderless now that Bacdir was gone, they would soon surrender. . . . Without further hesitation, Tiadann took the risk of launching into the Incl pocket tiny spheres containing the insidious product he had synthesized aboard the spaceship.

The effects were soon felt. In the twinkling of an eye the first ranks lay down their arms and the rest of the army soon followed suit.

The volatile product had only a short life, but in spite of her surprise Liane lost no time. She ordered her troops to advance among the heaps of corpses and weapons strewn on the thick grass. In this way many of the dazed Incls were taken prisoner before they realized what had happened to them.

Moruns also profited from this uphoped-for opportunity, and his knights were soon able to join forces with Liane's companies.

At this point, Tiadann noticed that the tide was rising, and sailing toward the river once more, he had no trouble reaching the banks occupied by the Lonkian troops. His shallops proceeded upriver, while he boarded one of the larger ships to rejoin the Lonkian leaders.

Just then a disturbing phenomenon occurred: a sphere of fire descended from the clouds and whirled around over the battlefield like an enormous will o' the wisp. The Lonks immediately decided that it could only be the Archangel Lignel come in person to demonstrate his pleasure with his faithful servants. Later, some of them even swore that they could distinctly make out his features and his diaphanous wings.

However, Tiadann was not fooled. "Well, my dear professor," he signaled to the phantasmagoric vision, "what do you think of my military abilities? I don't want to make any self-flattering comparisons to the famous generals and admirals of history, but I think I have every right to be pleased with myself. . . ."

"Not bad. You seem to have managed well enough. The Incls are apparently beaten, and your beloved Liane is going to be able to rescue the Duke of Fnar. The only trouble is that quite a few people have been slaughtered to satisfy your boundless ambition. . . . The kingdom of Lonk is yours and you now control the island of the Incls. Are your dreams of hegemony finally satiated?"

"How little you know me, my friend! But I'm afraid that's because I haven't been very frank with you! I assure you that I don't want to become dictator of this planet."

"But that's exactly where you're heading! No doubt you now intend to attack the kingdoms on the continent?"

"That's right! I also plan to have the Lonks occupy

that vast unexplored continent to the west, beyond the seas."

"Damnation! Your empire will be enormous. . . ."

"You mustn't think that I'm working toward some mean-spirited goal. On the contrary; I plan to impose a single language on all the inhabitants of Noldaz, and in that way peace will reign on the planet and scientific progress will be faster. In short, I intend to spare these primitives the trials that the humanoid races generally have to undergo in the course of their evolution. The Imperial government has demonstrated unbelievable cynicism in prohibiting interference with the development of these peoples. I want to prove that this attitude is not constructive. When I have shown that the peoples of primitive planets can be helped to attain a peaceful form of civilization rapidly, the Imperial inspectors will have to revise their position. Believe me or not as you wish, but I am conducting an important experiment that may very well completely change how we do things in the Galaxy. Once Noldaz has been pacified, I will withdraw!"

"Well, those are noble sentiments, indeed! I give you my word that if you had let me know what you were up to sooner, I might very well have softened my attitude. I hope you're successful. If things work out for you, the glory will be all yours. Have no illusions, however: the Galactic Inspectors will think twice before changing their attitude—though if you keep people from slaughtering themselves with atomic bombs in the future, you will obviously have demonstrated the value of your argument! Good luck! As for me, I'm going back to my theoretical studies—and by the way, I would appreciate it if you would send me a few more psychic tapes. I've almost run through those you were kind enough to place at my disposal."

"Of course! I'll see to it. . . ."

With these words the conversation came to an end. The professor soared into the heavens and could soon no longer be seen by the survivors of the battle.

Pleased with having convinced his ex-colleague of the purity of his intentions, Tiadann disembarked from his ship and, mounting a superb Incl steed, started off toward the tents over which waved the banners of the Lonkian chiefs. When he had raised the hanging that covered the entrance, he saw Ardez, Moruns, and Liane enjoying a hearty meal.

"Ah, here's our grand admiral," exclaimed the bastard, setting down the ham that he had been tearing into.

"Sit alongside me, my friend!" said Ardez, signaling an equerry to bring a stool. "It's been a rough day, hasn't it?"

"It has indeed, but victory has crowned our efforts. For my part, I have defeated the Incl fleet. Our lines of communication with the continent are open. Unfortunately, I had a little trouble with the fireships, and that held me up somewhat. Suddenly I found that I could no longer back up your troops on shore. But tell me what happened. . . . Apparently you've liquidated Rog Bacdir's army?"

"You can say that again," laughed Liane's equerry, pulling his nose out of a bowl of hotchpotch. "We beat hell out of those accursed dogs. But for a time there I was really sweating blood!"

"If it weren't for my brave Renouard, I probably would not be here with you this evening," interrupted the Maid. "On the right wing, we weren't able to carry the day. At one point I was even in great trouble. Luckily, Moruns completely shattered the opposing wing and the Incls melted away. We've taken more than ten thousand prisoners. All in all, it was less bloody than I feared it would be. If the encircled Incls had decided to die rather than surrender, our losses would have been heavy. . . ."

"It's too bad Bacdir slipped out of our grasp," noted Ardez. "He's probably on the way to the capital to organize its defense."

"Oh, they can't have many more men left," Moruns mumbled with a full mouth. "We'll lay siege to Linr and the place won't hold out long."

"Unless Rog Bacdir manages to raise a new army in the northern provinces," the Maid pointed out. "I'm afraid that we haven't seen the last of him. . . . In any case, I fear for our good Duke of Fnar. What will we do if the Incls threaten to kill him?"

"I have my own opinion about that!" exclaimed Tiadann. "We have to strike while the iron is hot. Listen to my plan. Normally, we would wait here for the arrival of reinforcements and supplies. . . ."

"We even ought to take over another port," the bastard interjected. "There's not much ammunition left, and half of our cavalry has no mounts. We need horses."

"Exactly what Bacdir will think!" replied the grand admiral with a sly smile. "Well, I think that we have to load our crack troops on the barges and go upriver to Linr immediately. The bottom is deep enough for our ships to sail right up to the capital. We can be there in two days. The Incls won't have had time to organize a defense. Our galliots will fire a few balls at the city, and I'll wager that the Incls will be so astonished to see us so soon that they'll give up without a fight. . . ."

"By my faith, I like your suggestion!" approved Liane. "If we do that, we can avoid unnecessary loss of life."

"If you ask me," objected Ardez, "I think the risk's too great."

Jealous of his own authority, the duke didn't look too kindly on the grand admiral's growing influence over Liane.

"What happens if our troops can't take the capital? The Incls will move in downstream and our forces will be isolated, cut off from supplies! We run the risk of a catastrophe!"

"Obviously, it's a big risk," said Moruns, setting the ham bone down in his bowl. "Nevertheless, I can't help liking the idea! That way we could get the whole business over with for good and all. We could capture King Dronz and liberate the Duke of Fnar without meeting any serious opposition! I'm for it!"

"It's pure madness!" stormed Ardez, bringing his fist down on the table.

His beard bristling, he looked furious; for the first time, the Lonkian leaders were in disagreement. The affair that had begun so well seemed on the point of turning nasty. . . . Ever prudent, Tiadann plunged his hand into his pocket and turned on his psycho-inductor while Liane was exclaiming:

"Well, I'm sorry, Ardez. You'll just have to accept the idea! Are you blind? Didn't you all see how the Archangel Lignel in person floated over our victorious army? I tell you true: the powers of Heaven speak from my mouth and Tiadann's. If it weren't for us, you would still be at Wronais at the court of Dauphin Sranz, who would never have been anointed king. As Moruns has pointed out, Tiadann's plan has many advantages. It saves human lives and makes it possible for us to free the Duke of Fnar. . . ."

"And what's more, it will make it impossible for Bacdir to raise a new army," Moruns continued. "The news of the capture of Linr will kill all desire to continue the struggle. The island will be quickly pacified. Until now, following the counsel of Liane and Tiadann has brought us nothing but triumph . . . Why do you hesitate?"

"That's telling him!" put in Renouard in a low voice. "Everybody is ready to obey the Maid! If she gave the word, I'd go to the end of Noldaz. . . ."

Ardez sighed deeply. The psycho-inductor waves were beginning to have an effect. "I have to admit that up to now you've done a magnificent job and that we've had no reason to regret having followed the advice of the gentle Maid," he grumbled, intentionally ignoring Tiadann. "Be it as she will, since Heaven chose her to enlighten us. However, if the business ends badly, don't say I didn't warn you. . . ."

Agreement having been reached and the meal finished, the Lonkian leaders separated to rest in their respective tents. The days to come were once more to be rich in memorable events.

Chapter Eight

The sun rose the next day in a serene sky. Delicate orange-red tints in the clouds promised a beautiful day.

A veritable human anthill swarmed over the riverbanks; while the men of arms tightened helmet gorgets and armor, the first echelons boarded the Lonkian barks. The greater part of the army was to sail upriver toward the capital and invest it as Tiadann had planned. There was no sign of the Incls, for what was left of their fleet had sought refuge on the northeast coast, and the survivors of the army, among them Rog Bacdir, were fleeing north across the sleeping countryside.

The grand admiral had slept badly: lascivious dreams had disturbed his rest. How surprised he was! What? Was this vulgar human phenotype, this contemptible castoff form of being, to be allowed to impose its sensual needs on him? He could, of course, have disconnected his neurons, but the learned historian let himself be enraptured by the charms of the senses as though he were some ordinary inhabitant of Noldaz. . . .

Alterdo had been fond of the local gastronomy, and Tiadann too liked to sample delicate dishes. Good vintages induced an agreeable euphoria in him. But what he was experiencing now troubled him deeply: when he thought of Liane, he felt an infinite tenderness accompanied by extremely curious yearnings.

The human part of him wanted desperately to press the young girl's soft, warm body against his own. He would have liked to smell the amber scent of her flesh, to caress her soft brown hair as he murmured tender words in her ear. But it was simply out of the question for a citizen of the Galactic Empire to enter into a long relationship with one of these short-lived creatures!

Needless to say, Tiadann had known the carnal love of light women, well-rounded chambermaids, but what he felt now was something very different. . . . When he walked up to the Maid, who was waiting before the gangplank of the ship that was to take them to Linr, she gave him a radiant smile that sharpened his desire.

Never had Liane looked at a Lonk that way.

Even Renouard seemed to notice: he coughed in embarrassment and began feverishly arranging his equipment.

Suddenly the Extraterrestrial understood. Everything was clear: she loved him, and he felt the same way about her. If this was so, why be troubled by scruples? There was no reason not to marry this valiant girl and have children by her. . . . Of course, one day he would have to leave Noldaz, but meanwhile he could lead a happy life alongside Liane.

On the condition, of course, that the Lonks would be willing to see their heroine lose her virginity: all primitive civilizations attached a mystic importance to the fact that creatures selected by their gods to play unusual roles should be innocent of sex. But after all, wasn't he too a divine messenger—one who had come to bring peace to this planet?

Embarrassed by the long silence, Liane had become all pink. Tiadann finally decided to make some commonplace statement.

"The heavens continue to smile down on us, gentle lady! What a wonderful day. . . . I hope you slept well!"

"My friend, I scarcely closed an eye last night. I thought so long of what you had said that the Archangel Lignel finally did me the honor of a visit. Perhaps he was jealous. . . ."

"Alas, sweet Maid, there would be no reason for him to be jealous of me. Since I've been fighting for the kingdom of Lonk, I have enjoyed very little of your pleasant company. . . ."

"Well, at least we will have some time to get to know each other better during the voyage to Linr. We have so much in common: Heaven has chosen us to guide my compatriots, and we have always been preoccupied by the same things. No shadow has ever darkened our relationship. When we spoke yesterday, I completely understood your desire to save human lives. That hulking Moruns thinks only of fighting! How glad I am to have finally been able to convince him to follow your counsel."

"Many thanks, Liane. My sole ambition, as you very well know, is to bring a lasting peace to Noldaz, and our task is far from over. . . ."

"Fear not, gentle friend. I will always be at your side, and nothing will ever separate us. The Archangel Lignel has impressively demonstrated his approbation. Henceforth, we will fight side by side!"

"How these words cheer me! That is my dearest desire, too."

Hearing this, the Maid gave him an enchanting smile and, drawing near, slipped her tiny hand into the soldier's rough palm.

Thus hand in hand they boarded the ship, where the captain was beginning to grow impatient. Behind them, Renouard opened eyes as big as saucers at this unusual sight, but the gruff equerry was smiling to himself. Apparently, this nascent idyll was in no way displeasing to him. Among the Lonks, the reputation of the grand admiral had continued to grow, and an alliance between their heroine and this valorous leader had a romantic aspect that appealed to them.

Of course, the Prince of Ardez might not feel the same way about it. . . .

All day long the cargo boats, pulled by robust teams following the towpath, continued up the river while squadrons of cavalry went ahead as scouts. As for the galliots, they had unfurled their sails and, taking advantage of a favorable wind, were moving under their own power.

Liane and Tiadann did not separate for so much as a moment, and spent the time exchanging commonplaces with infinite tenderness. They remained silent for long periods of time, clinging to each other lovingly, intoxicated by the warm odors emanating from the surrounding countryside.

Ardez was busy directing his knightly squadrons on the banks and therefore saw nothing. Moruns and Renouard, however, quietly seated on the bridge before a flask of wine, kept exchanging knowing looks and seemed quite moved by the spectacle.

Everyone knows that lovers are alone in the world: the two turtledoves, isolated in a marvelous universe, seemed to have forgotten completely that they were leading an expedition of war. It wouldn't have taken much for them to ask to be put ashore so that they could gambol in the green fields that offered a pastoral decor so suitable to the sweet games of love . . .

When evening came, the Maid and her faithful knight rejoined the marshal and the equerry and supped in their compnay. The ships had stopped in a verdant bend of the river and were awaiting a propitious moment to continue their journey by night so that they could get to the Incl capital as quickly as possible.

Under the starry sky, the fires that had been lit on the banks seemed part of a dream. Insects chirped in the tall grass, and frogs made the night reverberate with cries that sounded in the lovers' ears like silver bells.

The two turtledoves ate little; their eyes never left each other for a moment. Sometimes they sighed deeply, knees searching under the table to press against one another.

As for Moruns and Renouard, they conscientiously devoured their cassoulet, appreciating the culinary art of the ship's cook. From time to time they would launch a spicy pleasantry as they drank down a large swallow of wine, but the two other guests seemed not to hear them.

That night, when everybody retired to his cabin, for the first time in months Renouard did not take up his post across the threshold of the Maid's door. He remained leaning over the rails, dreamily contemplating the stars . . .

The Lonkian leaders demonstrated the same discretion, and as a result nobody knew for sure what happened between the two lovers, but it wasn't until late in the morning that the latter rejoined their friends.

Liane looked radiant, overflowing with the joy of

life. Tiadann was a bit pale and drawn and seemed to be sunk in the most profound bliss. They didn't quit each other's side for a moment, and they appeared to be linked in an almost supernatural understanding. They exchanged few words but were apparently able to read each other's thoughts in their eyes, as though by a sort of mutual complicity based on a total community of ideas.

As soon as their morning meal was over, both went to lean over the prow, shoulder to shoulder, silently contemplating the little waves that clapped against the sides of the ship.

Meanwhile, Moruns and Renouard were growing uneasy: the fleet was drawing near Linr, and already the galliots' bombards had thundered several times in reply to fire from light pieces along the banks.

As for Ardez, who was proceeding on land, whenever the river flowed through towns or villages, he had to fight a few skirmishes with squads that had been cut off from the main Incl body. He sent a messenger asking for details of the operation so that he might know if he was to force his way into the capital or merely isolate it by sending squadrons to take up positions before each of the city's gates.

Moruns was worried, and pensively scratching his head, he said to Renouard in perplexity, "As I live and breathe! They don't even hear the cannon anymore. . . . Should I take command?"

"With all due respect, marshal, I think it would be better to hear what the grand admiral has in mind. From what I understood, he wanted to lead his vessels in a surprise attack, and—well, you don't know much about ships. . . ."

"That's exactly what worries me. All right, come what may, I'm going to break that up. . . ."

The marshal strode off toward the prow with a firm step, and giving Tiadann a friendly tap on the shoulder, he exclaimed:

"My friend, I don't want to be indiscreet, but I'd appreciate it if you'd come back down to earth with the rest of us mortals. Look. There are the walls of Linr in the distance. It's high time that you told us what your plans are. Ardez in particular would like to know if he's to force his way through. He has nothing with which to lay siege and he'd like to know how to get through those thick walls surrounding the city. . . ."

"My apologies, Moruns!" replied his friend. "I was living through moments so marvelous that I had forgotten all about our problems. What's our present situation?"

"Ardez's squadrons have followed along the banks and are now near Linr, but the walls are an impregnable obstacle, given the slender means at his disposal."

"That's true!" said the admiral, suddenly becoming the man of action so admired by Moruns. "Of course it's out of the question for Ardez to try to penetrate the city. Send him this dispatch ordering him to take up a position before the gate closest to the river and wait. It's the fleet that's to carry the day for us. Here are my orders. . . ."

Renouard swiftly turned the dispatch over to a courier, who immediately disembarked. Meanwhile, Tiadann was saying:

"Two thick towers linked by chains guard the river entrance to Linr. The galliots are to moor nearby and bring those towers under heavy artillery fire. While this is going on, men from the armed shallops will cut through the links of the barrier with sledgehammers. As soon as the way is clear, our barks will haul the hookers and the skiffs to the principal bridge joining the two sections of Linr. At this point, our men will jump onto the bridge from the tops of the masts. When the artillery has softened up the enemy, the skiffs will draw up to the shore and disembark our troops, who will then be in a position to take the defenders of the wall from behind. Whatever the cost, they will have to capture the towers defending the gate before which Ardez will be waiting for us. As for you, you'll be in charge of the bridge. All you have to do is make sure that no reinforcements can pass over to the bank on which we will be fighting. Liane and I will accompany the men disembarking on the south bank."

"Understood!" agreed the marshal, delighted to see that his friend had recovered his usual dynamism. "I'll start for the galliots. . . ."

The operation went off without any serious difficulties. As Tiadann had foreseen, the Incls had not expected their adversaries to arrive before the capital so soon. They had received no reinforcements; all the available troops having been sent to the landing beaches, garrison manpower was down to a skeletal force and the artillery all but nonexistent. In addition, Rog Bacdir had not yet had time to reach Linr. King Dronz was still in his palace, and the Duke of Fnar in a cell of the famous tower prison where captives of noble lineage were kept.

Bombard fire from the galliots spread incredible panic: anguished burghers rushed down into their cellars to hide their treasures; terrified courtiers hastily mounted their carriages; in the palace, the royal councillors were pleading with the young sovereign and the queen mother to fly toward the north through those gates that were still free. But Dronz didn't like leaving his treasure behind: he gave orders for a column of heavy wagons to be loaded and could not bring himself to leave his palace until the vehicles were piled high.

Alas! He had waited too long. Sailors from the Lonkian barks had managed to cut the river chains as planned. Protected by the galliots, Moruns' skiffs had reached the bridge. Dropping from the rigging under the protection of arbalester fire, the men seized the two fortified towers at either end of the bridge.

From then on, there was nothing to prevent the Maid's elite troops from disembarking. Like demons spawned in hell, the Lonks, following Liane's banner, swarmed through the narrow streets, clashing with the garrison troops that tried to beat them back.

In this way, they reached the south gate, before which Ardez and his cavalry squadrons pawed the ground impatiently. The heavy drawbridge was raised, the portcullis pulled up, and the knights in turn erupted into Linr.

Meanwhile, part of the prince's troops had gone off to take up positions before the other gates, so the capital was completely cut off. Thus it was that Dronz had to turn around and head back to the palace.

New reinforcements continuously landing on the quais swelled the ranks of the Lonks. The entire southern section of the city was occupied in a few hours.

Liane and Tiadann had the honor of capturing Dronz himself. The sovereign had decided to comport himself as behooved his rank: wearing his crown, he greeted the assailants from his throne in the great audience chamber of the palace. A few minutes later a squad of arbalesters forced the entrance to the prison and liberated the Duke of Fnar who, brought to the palace, fell into the Maid's arms. . . .

Only the north bank still resisted. Moruns therefore traversed the bridge, and the unleashed Lonks liquidated the last defenders. By nightfall the entire capital was in the hands of the invaders. The king and the queen mother were prisoners—something that had never happened in the history of the island. . . .

And since success never comes singly, another even more extraordinary thing happened while the Lonkian leaders were celebrating their victory in the great hall. A detachment of knights presented themselves before the ramparts at the west gate. As the guards hesitated to open it, the leader of the troop himself came before the drawbridge and demanded to be allowed into the city.

The Lonks took counsel among themselves and decided to have one of the Incl prisoners call down agreement to this demand. And so it was that Rog Bacdir, the hated leader of the Incl armies that had spread fire and bloodshed through the kingdom of Lonk, was taken prisoner. Disarmed before he could realize what was happening, he was led before the Lonkian leaders, who couldn't get over the fact that even as they sat feasting they had captured their most ferocious enemy.

"Well, the whole family's here," laughed Ardez. "King Dronz will appreciate this visit by his valiant general! Bacdir, the roles have apparently been reversed: not too long ago you almost conquered the Lonks!"

"It's the chances of war. The outcome of a battle often depends on some little thing. If I had managed to get reinforcements during the siege of Fnar, things would be very different now!" replied the Incl leader in faultless Lonkian.

"Don't forget the Maid," Moruns called out at this point. "If Liane hadn't known how to make us all pull together, we would never have been able to liberate our country. You've always underestimated her. . . ."

"I admit as much. I even think that the time has come to present her with my apologies. My replies to her peaceful messages were not always notable for their courtesy," said the general, bowing before Liane. "Perhaps I failed to understand her. . . ."

"You may be assured of my pardon!" replied the lady. "Understand this, Bacdir. I wanted to free the kingdom of Lonk, have my king crowned, and liberate the Duke of Fnar. I have achieved all three goals. The mission confided in me by the Archangel Lignel is finished, insofar as the Lonks are concerned. In spite of that, I don't feel that my work is done. We have too intimately known the horrors of war; this plague must disappear from Noldaz! My celestial voices have so ordered, and they have confirmed as much to my dear Tiadann. Henceforth, peace must reign between all nations, and our mission will not be complete until this goal has been attained. Only then, Bacdir, will we be able to take our well-deserved rest!"

"What you say is very praiseworthy, gentle lady, but I would like to hear from your own mouth the means by which you envisage making peace reign between our kingdoms," replied the prisoner. "In former times, dictators tried to impose a despotic government by force of arms; they failed because of the unshakeable resistance of the conquered peoples."

"We are perfectly aware of the complexities of the problem," Tiadann interjected at this point. "If we evacuate your island, our interests must inevitably diverge one day or another, and the fighting will begin all over again. Believe me, we have no desire to enslave you; we want to respect your customs and your national culture—but our troops will remain here as long as is necessary. Only linguistic unity can bring about real comprehension among the inhabitants of Noldaz. Your religion itself emphasizes the fact that your god, wanting to punish the inhabitants of this planet, created a situation in which the peoples stopped speaking a common language.

"It had been my intention to impose Lonkian as a universal language. Upon reflection, however, it seems to me that that would be an error. No local idiom can fulfill this role. I have therefore chosen an ancient dialect used by the priests of your religion. Your schools will be obliged to teach both languages. In this way, the peoples of this planet will have a common means of communication, and once this happens, many false problems will cease to separate them!"

"Easy enough to say! You must be joking, sir. If I have understood you, we are to remain under Lonkian occupation for an indeterminate time. You will probably name a regent, just as we did for the Lonks, and your sovereign will have himself anointed king of the Incls! Never will we accept such tyranny!"

"Which is exactly why we have no intention of imposing it upon you!" interjected the admiral. "Liane and I have long argued the question, and subject to acceptance by King Sranz, here is what the new status of your country will be. Moruns will be our sovereign's delegate to your young King Dronz. He will in no way interfere in the governing of the island. We only ask that several Incl contingents come to join some of our troops who are on the point of setting out on a vast crusade to the countries occupied by the infidels. Together, we will see to it that the peoples of Noldaz learn to speak a single language: Noldazian. A delegate from each country participating in this crusade will be placed near each local sovereign to assure that he no longer maintains an army and that he does indeed have Noldazian taught. In this way, peace will reign on Noldaz!"

"This condition seems very strange to me," Rog Bacdir said in some perplexity. "But all in all, you appear sincere, even though I don't really understand the importance of this universal language. However, you, Liane, have apparently received orders from the celestial powers. . . . In the beginning, I admit that I took the Maid for a shameless adventuress, but now I confess my error: each of her predictions has come true, point by point. . . ."

"Will you agree to be our spokesman to your king?" asked Liane.

"I think I will be acting for the greater good of all peoples if I do. Fighting side by side, our two nations, which have learned to fear each other, will learn to esteem each other. The same will be true of other countries."

"All that's fine and grand!" exclaimed Ardez. "But what about the vast countries stretching to the east and the north? Never will the fierce emperor who governs them agree to have this Noldazian of yours taught in his schools, and still less to have a watchdog committee of Incls and Lonks at his side! We will have to war against him for years, and that empire is immense. . . ."

"We will at least be in a position to propose a treaty with him," Tiadann pointed out. "The union of the Lonks, Xovians, and Incls represents the elite of Noldaz chivalry. The emperor of the north will think twice before rejecting our propositions—I am willing to wager on it!"

"What do you have to say about all this, Liane?" asked Moruns.

"I agree with Tiadann completely. Before every battle with the Incls I first proposed a peaceful solution of our differences. . . ."

"Which I was wrong to reject!" Bacdir noted. "I underestimated the power of the celestial forces guiding the Maid. To tell the truth, I didn't believe in them at all! But now the facts are clear. The emperor will have to recognize that the Archangel Lignel truly speaks from the mouth of your heroine."

"Well," thought the Extraterrestrial to himself. "You can be sure that I'll do what's necessary to convince him of that. . . . I no longer give a damn about the Galactic Inspectors: things have gone too far for me to turn back now. . . ."

"God be praised!" rejoiced Liane. "May I now propose that our valorous adversary take his place beside us and share a meal in friendship?"

"Willingly! It will be the first public demonstration of the reconciliation of our peoples."

And thus it was that hostilities between the Incls and the Lonks came to an end in an Homeric banquet. So many reciprocal toasts were drunk to the courage of the valiant combatants that in the morning all the gallant knights were snoring soundly under the tables. Renouard had wisely escorted the Maid to her chamber so that she might be spared the transports of her tipsy compatriots. . . .

Of course, long rivalry between certain fiercely nationalistic nobles and their sovereign resulted in additional clashes. Some of the nobles even openly rebelled. Joint expeditions, however, soon brought the hotheads to a rightful understanding of the facts. Moruns showed himself skillful enough not to be cruel or vindictive, and there were no executions. Only a few counts were stripped of their powers, and other Incls—never a Lonk—replaced them.

Following Tiadann's regulations, innumerable new schools were created. They were tuition-free and offered instruction by learned teachers chosen from among the monks. Even the most humble had the right to an education. In the beginning, the sons of nobles scorned these establishments, but since the king insisted that command of the universal language was a prerequisite for any official post, the lords were soon forced to send their offspring to study alongside commoners. And thus little by little the gap separating the two peoples disappeared.

During this time, Tiadann continued his mission of pacification. The grand admiral had left Linr in the company of Liane, Ardez, and the Duke of Fnar the day after the capital was taken. Supplies came directly up the river, and there were no longer any problems on this account. A new task awaited the savant, however: he had to persuade King Sranz to lead a crusade against the infidels of the South. But before doing that he had to be assured of the collaboration of the Emperor of the North, who had remained neutral during the fighting.

The channel crossing was made without incident, and Liane and Tiadann took full advantage of the few hours of tranquillity. Even the weather was their ally, and the sun shone during the entire voyage. The Lonkian heroine scarcely parted from the man she loved with all her soul. Side by side on the bridge, the two lovers surrendered their satiated bodies to the caresses of the sea breeze and forgot all about their troubles.

They would willingly have sailed along like that for months.

Ardez was fully aware of their relationship now, but he appeared to accept it and behaved very discreetly. When the ship reached the mouth of the Rifen, the lieutenant general chose to disembark with the Duke of Fnar and gallop to Aniar at top speed. He was intent on being the first to report the expedition's success to King Sranz and, as usual, to assign himself the lion's role in events.

The two lovers were well above such shabby sentiments. They blissfully traveled up the river on a barge pulled by a team of peaceful oxen, and they passed their time engaged in the kind of small talk standard in such situations, untiringly repeating the litanies of happy lovers.

Tiadann was also trying to complete the education of his companion, depicting for her the immensity and ineffable beauties of the universe. . . . His dearest desire would have been to free Liane from her fragile body and confer on her a life as long as his own—to make the little peasant girl a citizen of the Galactic Empire. Alas, this was beyond his powers.

His pupil, though astonished, proved extremely receptive; for example, in contemplating the glimmering "fireflies" in the sky, she learned to recognize the constellations and the neighboring planets that turned around the same sun that Noldaz did. But it took all her love to make her accept that Noldaz was spherical in form: wasn't that a heresy denounced by the priests?

Perhaps she even began to suspect that her companion had not learned of all these marvels from the Archangel Lignel. If she did, she gave no sign of it.

For his part, Tiadann never confessed his origins to

her, though he was often sorely tempted. Later—he thought—he could take her aboard the spaceship. But how could he ever explain to her his real bodily form, a form that in no way corresponded to his present aspect? How could he confess that he might very well live for hundreds of years, even though her life was a short one?

When the barge docked in Aniar, a crowd was there to welcome the Maid. An escort of knights and notables accompanied the two heroes to the palace as the spectators cheered untiringly and waved banners emblazoned with Liane's colors.

Everyone spoke of the great deeds of the humble shepherdess who had successfully carried out the seemingly impossible task she had set herself. Now the country was free, the Duke of Fnar liberated: every Lonk would have followed the Maid to the end of the world if she had asked him to.

King Sranz VII received his honored guests in his private cabinet. His uncle and Ardez were beside him, as were his advisers and ministers. When Liane and Tiadann came to kneel before him in sign of homage, he did them the unusual honor of rising and bestowing the accolade on them. Then, with a wave of his hand, the sovereign invited them to take their places in armchairs on either side of the throne.

"My dear child," he exclaimed; "Our dynasty will forever be in your debt! You have delivered Our kingdom from the Incl occupation and liberated the Duke of Fnar. How can We ever express Our gratitude to you? Nor are We forgetting the valorous leaders who faithfully seconded you. We especially have in mind Our loyal grand admiral, whose exploits made it possible to defeat the enemy fleet and disembark on the island of the Incls . . . Speak, gentle

Maid. Ask of me what you will, and by Our Holy Relics We solemnly promise to grant your desires!"

Tiadann, of course, had not failed to turn on his psycho-inductor as soon as he had entered the room. He was therefore not at all astonished to hear Liane reply:

"Sire, I have never undertaken anything without the counsel of my celestial voices, and I ask nothing for myself. The happiness of the Lonks is enough to fill my heart with joy. However, my task on earth is not over. The Archangel Lignel had ordered me to have you anointed king, to liberate the kingdom of Lonk, and to deliver the Duke of Fnar. These things are now done. But Lignel has spoken to me again, and he has also deigned to allow your faithful vassal Tiadann to hear his voice."

"This is marvelous news indeed," said the king enthusiastically. "And what did he order you to do?"

"Your Majesty, the heavenly powers allow that one may fight for a just cause," replied Liane. "Thus, many Lonks have suffered and perished to free their country. But such things must come to an end. Henceforth, the archangel—God's spokesman—desires war to be forever banished from Noldaz. . . ."

"We completely subscribe to these sentiments. Our people have sufficiently suffered the atrocities of war to aspire to a definitive peace. However, We reign only over Lonk. How can We impose Our will on other peoples?"

"That is exactly what I want to talk to you about. Tiadann and I have received precise instructions: henceforth the peoples will be united by a new bond—a universal language that will make it possible for men to understand one another better and that will put an end to their rivalries. Noldazian will be taught to all by learned monks."

"I can well understand your desire, Liane. I hope that this linguistic unity may indeed unite all the peoples of Noldaz, which is why upon the morrow I will sign a decree imposing its instruction in Xovia, among the Incls, and in My kingdom. But what will happen in the other countries?"

"We must dispatch messengers to the Emperor of the North and let him know that the Archangel Lig-nel commands contingents from all countries of be-lievers to undertake a crusade against the infidels of the South. He too will have to agree to have Noldazian taught in his schools. Your present power must make him fear you, and there is no doubt that he will accept. . . ."

"*Especially if I make a quick trip to my spaceship and have my oniro-suggestor inspire him with a few carefully chosen dreams,*" thought Tiadann secretly.

"By My faith, that is a noble and vast undertaking!" said Sranz pensively. "However, it seems to Us that the nobility of this celestial mission must be apparent to him. We therefore quite willingly agree to send an ambassador to Our noble imperial neighbor. But who will command this crusade?"

"Moruns will have to remain among the Incls for some time. I think that the Dukes of Fnar and Ardez are the right men to command our contingents. Each people will have its own leaders, but your uncle will be the generalissimo of all the armies."

"Don't you wish to take part in this great enter-prise?"

"No, Sire," Liane replied. "The Archangel has given me another mission. Noldaz, he has informed me, is not flat, as the ancient masters taught. Its form is that of a round fruit. Beyond the seas there is a vast continent peopled by primitives who know nothing of our holy religion. I therefore ask Your Majesty to permit Admiral Tiadann to lead an expedition that will traverse the oceans with a few of your ships. In that way we can convince the leaders of these tribes to render homage to the king of Lonk, and we can instruct them in the dogmas of our religion. Of course, Noldazian will also be taught overseas."

"Bless my soul! That's quite a story. . . . If We didn't have complete confidence in you, We would never be able to believe that men clamber about on a sphere! How can the inhabitants of the antipodes live upside down? How is it that the oceans do not spill into the surrounding space?"

"These are esoteric mysteries that the Archangel Lignel has confided to the noble Tiadann, who is more apt than a poor unlearned girl to understand such marvels. Our grand admiral would be honored if you would agree to look over a learned account explaining the whys and wherefores of these miracles."

"By all the saints, We will read it with great interest! You have demonstrated the veracity of your assertions, and your soul is pure, Liane, which is why We undertake to realize all your desires down to the smallest point. As soon as We ourselves and Our counselors have deciphered the grand admiral's documents, We will give him a fleet."

Tiadann bowed deeply and then, kneeling, turned over the dossiers he had prepared for the sovereign.

Sranz seized them with eager curiosity and immediately began leafing through the parchments. He was so involved in his reading that he neglected to reply to the farewells of Liane and Tiadann, who discreetly took their leave.

Chapter Nine

To tell the truth, the admiral and the Maid were beginning to lose interest in the affairs of the kingdom. Completely taken up with their mutual love, they were not at all eager to continue an adventurous life marked by incessant battles. The great crusade of the continental kingdoms would go on for a long time, and the commanders of the army would have to lead a number of expeditions. As admiral, Tiadann would have had to leave Liane often. For this reason both of them preferred to depart on a voyage of discovery aboard Lonkian ships—it guaranteed them against separation.

But there was also another reason: both were tired of battles and slaughter. They wanted peace. Tiadann had sworn to himself to make maximum use of incapacitants to prevent the infidels from setting up strong resistance. The mobility of his teleguided spaceship and the production capacity of its synthesizer made this possible for him to do—especially since there was still no sign of the Imperial inspectors. But he felt that he had done enough for the civilized peoples of Noldaz. He had set them a peaceful ideal and given them the technological means necessary to successfully conclude the union of the different nations. The common language would prevent them from returning to a cycle of wars, and the universal religion would surely lead them to live in understanding.

Tiadann was also well aware that as long as he dwelt among the Lonks he would never be able to marry Liane. To them, their heroine remained "the Maid," and these simple people would never understand if she were to marry like any ordinary girl in the kingdom.

When the admiral had taught the continentals to conquer the oceans, his role would be over. He could then settle down beyond the seas as a viceroy and finally wed Liane. The Lonks would no longer attach the same importance to it. Moruns and Fnar would soon gain new laurels as leaders of the crusade and nobody would give any more thought to Liane and her companion.

It remained to endow the Lonkian ships with the means of making a long sea voyage. Having received full powers from Sranz, Tiadann went about it with his usual competence. The modification of the rigging had made it easy to turn in the wind, and the compass provided a means of maintaining direction. If the mariners could measure the distance covered each day, they could navigate by dead reckoning.

To ascertain distance, the navigator made use of a log: he tossed a weighted plank into the sea, and a sailor would run out a line knotted at regular intervals. In this way it could be established how many "knots" a ship covered in an hour. But the Lonks still had to learn how to measure this lapse of time accurately. Of course, the sun could be used as a reference point when it was directly overhead—at noon—but this height varied with the latitude. . . .

After checking through the archives, the galactic

savant discovered that the clepsydra was known to the peoples of the South. Evidently this water clock was not ideal for use on board a constantly moving ship, but it was better than nothing. Thanks to its indications, more precise than those of an hour glass, the mariners would be in a position to determine longitude. Later, the admiral would furnish them with escapement pendula which would be considerably more exact. For the moment, the clepsydra would do, especially since—thanks once again to his spaceship—Tiadann knew the distance to be sailed and the direction to follow. The rest was a simple administrative problem.

The ships assembled in the Lonkian port farthest south received sufficient supplies for a year-long crossing: salted or smoke-cured meat, dried fish, biscuits, dried vegetables, cheese, wine, and a quantity of citrus fruits and onions to ward off scurvy. Noldazians, like most humanoids, were unable to synthesize vitamin C within their bodies.

Soon everything aboard the twenty expeditionary ships was ready. Certain sages in the king's court persisted in saying that the vessels would never come to another continent, since the planet was flat. They were convinced that the fleet would be brought up short at the edge of a bottomless abyss and that it might very well fall into space; but Sranz, under the influence of the psycho-induction to which Tiadann had subjected him, refused to pay them any attention. The expedition therefore left as scheduled in the autumn following the Incl defeat.

Moruns, Ardez, and Fnar, who had been busy completing preparations for the crusade, came to see their friends off. They were all saddened to be losing companions in arms whose value they had learned to appreciate, but they were also extremely curious to find out if Tiadann had told the truth: was their planet really a sphere?

Bedecked with multicolored flags and bearing Liane's banner atop the main mast, the ships were soon sailing past the fort situated on the extreme promontory of the continent. Bombards thundered out their salutes and the vessels resolutely headed west.

A few hours later the thin gray line of the coast had disappeared and the expedition was alone on the immense expanse of ocean.

"Ah, my treasure," grumbled the faithful Renouard, "I would never have believed there could be so much water. . . . If my poor mother could see me now! When I was a child, she was always worried that I'd drown in our village stream!"

"Do stop complaining, my good fellow!" Liane scolded gently. "You know that the Archangel Lignel gave the admiral precise instructions on the route to be sailed. Look at me—I've scarcely gotten my sea legs, and I'm as comfortable as if I were in my native village."

"That's fine for you! But I don't understand a thing about all this nonsense. . . . If our ship is sailing on a big ball, we'll soon have our feet in the air—and then how will we keep from falling off?"

"Don't worry about it," interrupted Tiadann. "Did you see our compass?"

"Of course—that little gadget that always points in the same direction. . . ."

"That's the one. Well, the forces that keep our feet on the bridge of this ship are as invisible as those that draw the needle north, and yet they exist and will keep us upright, even if we go to the antipodes on the other side of the ball."

"Ah, I see what you mean. . . . In that case I needn't sweat so! Since there's no risk of flying off into nothing, the admiral has my complete confidence!"

Upon which the faithful equerry went off to watch the sailors killing time by fishing off the stern.

"The fact is," sighed Liane, pressing up against Tiadann, "I pretend to be brave, but I'm not at all easy in my mind. All this is so new to me. In spite of my complete confidence in you, I just can't get used to the idea that beyond this vast ocean there are creatures like ourselves. . . . Did the archangel give you any details about them?"

"To tell the truth, very few. All I know is that they resemble us but live in an extremely primitive manner."

"And what sort of reception can we expect? Won't they be very frightened by our ships?"

"They'll most likely be bewildered by the sight of us. But the size of our vessels—and the bombards on them—can be counted on to inspire a healthy respect and incite them to deal peacefully with us."

"I hope so. . . ." sighed Liane. "I would find it very hard to have to return to the incessant fighting I so hate. Ah, I dream of a house on a hillside, with orchards all around, and just you and me. Later, perhaps, with children . . ."

"I too long for a peaceful existence, my darling! Nevertheless, we had better not count on being able to set up housekeeping as soon as we get there. I'll have to found colonies along the coast, at favorable sites. When enough small forts have been established, we will send our ships to bring the news back to King Sranz. We can also send a few presents that will inspire others to join us. When there are enough colonists, we will be able to enjoy a well-earned rest."

"Do you think these primitives are rich? Some navigators have made fortunes by bringing back spices, dyes, precious stones, and even gold from far-off countries. The sailors are counting on discovering immense treasures. . . ."

"It would be a mistake to rely on that. The lust for gain will only lead to wars against the natives, and that's not the purpose of our expedition. Our colonists will have to become farmers, raise cattle, and open up vast uncultivated lands. Sooner or later, of course, there will inevitably be friction with the aborigines, but we will have to learn how to deal fairly and live in peace with them. We must educate them and train administrators who will help us govern the country."

"And suppose they refuse to collaborate with us?"

"Initially some of them are sure to be unwilling, but when they have learned to know us there will be no problems. These lands are big enough to feed millions of people."

"Ah, I love to hear you talk that way! If only we can maintain peace among all the peoples . . ."

"Have confidence, Liane! With Heaven's help, we will establish a durable peace on Noldaz. . . ."

A cold wind blew from the north. Liane shivered and left her companion to warm herself in the cabin on the stern.

Before rejoining her, the admiral glanced around. The gracefully inclined ships were speeding west. A sailor kept watch on the prow. Aloft, lookouts searched the horizon. In the aftercastle the navigator was conscientiously playing out his log while another sailor noted on a tablet the number of knots slipping by.

Up front the crew was drowsing, snug and warm in the vast hold reserved to it. The hammocks—another of Tiadann's innovations—swayed back and forth like pendula. Nobody seemed in the least concerned. Reassured, the admiral went off to rejoin his companion with a satisfied smile: if the Galactic Inspectors had left him in peace for a few more months, he would have proved that it was possible to accelerate the evolution of a planet and spare it the painful trials that had until then accompanied the psychological maturation of primitives. . . .

After that there would be serene days alongside the woman he loved until she grew old and died. Then it would be time to reenter into contact with the galactic authorities. Unless, of course, Iern'an eventually found his stay too tedious and played some trick on his former assistant . . . For the time being, he was keeping quiet, but he must be aware of his ambitious colleague's new projects. Perhaps he was losing interest. . . .

The crossing continued monotonously, storms alternating with fine weather. Thanks to his aerial photographs, Tiadann could avoid the most serious weather disturbances, at least to the extent that his far from speedy ships allowed. He also saw to it that advantage was taken of favorable currents, which added somewhat to the ship's speed but considerably upset the calculations of the distance sailed.

The crew filled time with the usual shipboard operations: watching at the helm, splicing rope, repairing the sails, caulking the hull, scraping down the anchor chains and all the ship's metal parts. A periodic distribution of wine maintained morale, but still the men began to feel that time hung heavy on their hands. Divers strange phenomena occurred—for instance, the compass ceased pointing toward the star indicating the north. Unable to explain that the lines of magnetic force varied in different places, Tiadann declared that the star had moved in the sky.

Then flights of birds appeared. All the sailors were convinced that they were some kind of ducks, but actually they were seafowl. What they took for a sign of the proximity of land momentarily encouraged the members of the expedition, but they were disappointed in their hopes, and a gloomy despondency descended on the vessels.

There were also false alarms; on several occasions the lookouts cried "Land!" but the coast they had glimpsed was only a large cumulus whose shape suggested the summit of a snow-capped mountain.

Ten days after the departure from Lonk, another phenomenon spread panic on board: one night all the metallic parts of the ships were covered with sparks; balls of fire moved from one mast to the other. Obviously it was St. Elmo's fire, due to the discharge of static electricity. This time, Tiadann explained that these were manifestations of celestial angels who had chosen this way to make their presence known. Liane was not convinced, but she said nothing. A liberal distribution of wine put heart back into the sailors.

Alas, the very next day the expedition sailed right into a vast field of algae that covered the ocean as far as the eye could see. The wind fell completely and sails drooped from the masts.

This time the men were convinced that they had come to the end of their journey: they all knew that seaweed grew on coastal bottoms. A few fishermen even caught crabs, and this reinforced their conviction.

Tiadann was careful not to undeceive them. He

knew that this accummulation of seaweed was due to the marine current, but thanks to the photos taken by his spaceship, he also knew that nowhere in the region was there a prospect for good sailing winds. The expedition might very well be becalmed for some time.

Initially, the sailors took the situation well and even profited from the occasion to bathe and swim. Several of them came across bits of wood of an unknown kind, and this convinced them that the fleet was in the vast estuary of a river, especially since the water had a less briny taste.

A week later the situation remained unchanged.

The ships were still becalmed. In despair, the sailors had insisted on towing them by rowing the shallops. Given the fiery sun, these efforts were short-lived. Soon, all the men lay stretched gloomy and hopeless in the shade of the sails. Were they going to perish this way, far from their native land? True, there was no lack of food—the fishing had proved very good—but water was beginning to be in short supply and had to be rationed.

Liane suffered from the heat, and her morale started to decline. She became irritable and would snap at Tiadann for little or no reason.

Finally one night a light wind swelled the sails. The sea became wrinkled. Immediately, the sailors clambered up the masts to hoist the sails. Everybody began insisting that the expedition turn back, but the admiral remained inflexible. He even went so far as to threaten to hang the ringleaders, and things settled down without his having to use the oniro-suggestor.

For the next two days the ships moved swiftly westward with the wind in their sails. It was not quite so hot, but the men remained inert, overcome by a sense of fatality. They all thought that they were lost forever on a vast stretch of water containing not the least bit of land. . . .

Just about then the sailor in charge of the log fished up some seaweed and a piece of moss-covered wood. Everybody began to scan the surface of the sea, and soon they pulled up a leafy branch and even berries of some kind. This time the sailors were not mistaken: these were signs of nearby land. On top, the lookouts redoubled their attention. Flights of birds sped across the sky, indicating the direction of the coast; the ships followed them.

Then the long-awaited cry was heard: "Land!"

Cannon were fired and all eyes turned fixedly toward the gray line on the horizon. There was no possible doubt; the expedition had completed the crossing! Indescribable enthusiasm broke out on all the vessels.

As night was falling, the admiral hove to so that there would be no risk of his ships hitting a reef. He took advantage of the opportunity to get his exact bearings and check on whether they had only come to some island. But no, the satellite confirmed that he was off a large bay not far from a river.

At the crack of dawn, the fleet started up again, the shallops in the lead to sound the bottoms. And thus it came to a vast break in the coastline. Two rocky promontories enclosed a long sandy beach and luxuriant trees that formed a green mantle as far as the eye could see.

The time had come to establish contact with the aborigines. Since one false move might very well compromise all future relations with the natives of the region, Tiadann ordered everyone to unload his arms. He had some trinkets placed in the longboats, put on his most sumptuous uniform and, accompanied by Liane, stepped aboard a shallop that took him to the beach. The moment was an historical one: a new continent had been discovered. . . .

The arrival of the vessels had not gone unnoticed. The beach was swarming with "savages" clothed only in multicolored feather diadems, the fullness of which seemed intended to indicate rank.

Needless to say, Tiadann had supplied himself with a thought reader so that he could accurately judge the intentions of the welcoming committee. The encounter went off extremely well.

"Great balls of fire!" said Renouard, enraptured. "If my poor mother and father could see me with all these painted and plumed savages, they'd never get over it!"

"Let's remain calm and dignified," the admiral commanded his escort, ignoring the comment. "Don't make a move toward your weapons. The sailors carrying the gifts are to follow me but to distribute nothing without my order!"

When Tiadann set foot on land, the ships, as had been arranged, fired a gun salute. The rumbling detonations of the bombards sowed panic among the natives. Only the chief put on a bold front and stood his ground, awaiting his visitors. The others fled or threw themselves flat on the ground and hid their heads in their hands.

Admiral Tiadann stopped a few paces from the group of notables and gestured in greeting. His opposite number replied in the same way. Somewhat reassured, the savages got to their feet, staring at the Lonks in stupefaction: never would they have believed that men could control the thunder. . . .

On a sign from the chief's beribboned baton, two naked-breasted lissom girls came forward gracefully and set at Tiadann's feet baskets of reddish-brown fruits, bark basins of shellfish, and some extremely pretty necklaces of gold nuggets. The admiral bowed his thanks and, bending down, chose the most marvelous adornment and placed it around Liane's neck.

For some reason less terrified than the men, the women in the crowd stepped forward and presented the sailors with feathered headdresses, which they placed upon them with coquettish gestures.

Now that he had been rendered signs of homage, Tiadann could in turn distribute his gifts. The sailors, therefore, advanced and placed trunks of trinkets before the local monarch. Scorning the beaded necklaces, the ruler seemed most interested in the copper pots and plates. He seized one of them and began using it as a drum while his subjects went into a swaying dance to the music of conches and reedy flutes.

Meanwhile the Lonks had continued disembarking. A troop of harquebusiers took up position behind the admiral, while lightweight culverins and their ammunition were hauled up on the beach.

Oviously knowing nothing about firearms, the leader of the savages paid no attention. When the choreographic demonstration was over, the cortege reformed and the Lonks were invited to follow their guests to the village, which they did without further delay.

The settlement did not have houses with roofs of gold leaf, as some had expected, but was composed of simple bark huts covered with branches. Obviously the savages knew nothing about metallurgy. A primitive idol was enthroned in the large open space before the leader's dwelling: a larger hut paved with flat stones. Several spits were turning over a fire in the middle of the room. Crude seats of stretched animal skins had been set in a circle. And thus began the Lonks' first meal on the new continent, baptized Lianide, in honor of their heroine.

Thanks to Tiadann's translator, friendly relations were quickly established. The natives were quite taken with the metal household objects, the knives, and the flint lighters they received as gifts. They readily agreed to grant the strangers a neighboring promontory as their own, and there Tiadann built a small fortress made of logs; inside he set up a few artillery pieces.

By the end of a week or so, the Lianides couldn't get along without their new friends. They followed them about like dogs, and went into ecstacies when the Lonkian rifles brought down some large fowl.

In the beginning they were also surprised to see some of the Lonks clear a piece of land and work it with iron plowshares. Content to fish, gather wild fruit, and hunt in the game-rich forests, they had never so much as thought of using such methods to obtain food.

Soon the chief solemnly signed a treaty of friendship with the Lonks. But this was by no means the only notable event: yes, Liane finally married Tiadann in a quiet ceremony at which the ship's chaplain officiated.

As to the sailors, they didn't enter into formal marriages, but this did not inhibit them from establishing tender relations with the beautiful savage women. Careful not to carry any women on his ships, the galactic savant had counted on fast interbreeding by his men to create bonds of affection with the natives and inspire peaceful relations between the two communities—relations founded on friendly exchanges.

A fortnight after his arrival, the admiral decided

that the time had come to continue his exploration of the continent. He left behind a garrison of some hundred well-armed men. A swift ship supplied with fresh provisions departed for the kingdom of Lonk bearing a few samples of local products and two or three savages. Once this had been done, the rest of the expedition began a long coastal journey north.

A vast fertile region was discovered. There were few inhabitants, and they were almost always friendly: respectful of the strangers' powerful weapons, they were intent on insinuating themselves into the good graces of the Lonks. The latter established forts in various places and supplied each colony with seed and farming implements so that after the first harvest its autonomy could be assured.

The farther north the fleet went, the colder the weather became. In addition, the native tribes they encountered became fiercer: the savages were not only less outgoing but also looked different. These new tribes led a nomadic existence and hunted on the vast plains. Horsemen, mounted on extremely swift hexapod steeds, followed the ships up the coast. Inevitably, the first clashes occurred.

According to a now well-organized technique, the expedition had just established a fort near a magnificent, fish-filled lake. Tiadann was getting ready to return to his ships when a scout signaled that a horde of aborigines was galloping up. Since the ships were too far off to intervene, all the admiral could do was mew up his men behind the wooden ramparts.

"This time," Renouard grumbled, "we're going to have to make use of our harquebuses."

"I hope not," sighed Liane. "It would be a pity to begin fighting these poor people. Everything has been going so well!"

"We will not initiate hostilities," Tiadann said. "That's all I can promise you. But this time the natives seem determined to drive us away. . . ."

In the account that he gave of the colonization of the New World, the chaplain of the fleet related the following:

"The gates had hardly been closed behind our last men when the cavalry charge broke against our walls. These painted demons were uttering discordant cries. Riding up to the ramparts, they let fly a hail of arrows and then, wheeling about, sped away.

"A few Lonks were very seriously wounded, and the Maid immediately tended to them. Still the admiral hesitated to shed blood. He gave orders for the culverins to be aimed at a thicket of trees to the right of the savage leaders.

"The gunners obeyed, and the balls soared through the air and cut down the trunks, which fell with a clatter.

"There was a clear movement of retreat among the assailants. Then two warriors, their chests striped with white, came to examine the tree trunks and in astonishment ran their fingers over the splinters of wood.

"The admiral then gave orders for a second salvo to be fired at a group of horses kept in reserve. This time the raking fire disemboweled some ten of the unfortunate animals. In some perplexity, the chiefs went again to inspect the damage.

"Alas, the lesson was not enough to bring them to their senses: the troop got up on the surviving horses and came to launch flaming arrows at the fort. Water had to be drawn from the lake to put out the fire.

"The savages repeated this performance several times, charging, firing, then beating a retreat. Our admiral was beginning to have enough."

(The fact is that Tiadann had left his psycho-inductor aboard his flagship and didn't even have with him the tele-control for his satellite.)

"This time the culverins were loaded with case shot, and when the tight ranks of assailants were a short distance away the guns spit forth their iron pellets with a deafening roar.

"When the smoke had cleared, a terrible spectacle greeted our eyes. Dozens of dead and wounded lay stretched upon the ground. Their companions, wild with terror, were galloping away in retreat, and were not seen again for a long time.

"As was her custom, Liane had given orders for the enemy wounded to be tended to. Some thirty of them were still alive. They couldn't understand why their enemies didn't finish them off: these poor savages knew nothing of the precepts of charity. . . .

"However, this good deed was not forgotten. Afterward, when our colonists re-entered into contact with their former enemies, the latter had high esteem for them, and especially for the thunder spit forth by their iron tubes. The wounded who had been treated by our men assured their compatriots of our peaceful intentions. A land grant was made to the Lonks and the treaty signed was never broken.

"Continuing their voyage, the Maid and our admiral completed the colonization of the region by establishing other coastal trading centers. In this way we soon reached the glacial regions. The sea was swollen with fish of all kinds; there were also monsters that frightened us sorely, and in addition, the rough climate disheartened our men, who were used to the warmth of their native land.

"The expedition therefore turned and redescended

the coast toward our point of departure. At each colony the admiral left a few ships loaded with provisions so that a regular liaison could be set up between our divers establishments.

"Thanks to celestial protection, the return voyage was made under favorable circumstances. And so concludes the account, as exact as possible on all points, of the first contacts of the Lonks with the New World. The second volume of this history will be dedicated to the development of our colonies in peaceful understanding with the natives. May the Archangel Lignel, who has guided us, be praised down the centuries. . . ."

Now that Tiadann had completed his task, he wanted to settle in a pleasant region and live there with his beloved Liane. But he could not lose all interest in what was happening on the other side of the ocean.

As soon as he was properly established on his charming farm, in a region inhabited by the friendly people who had been discovered first, he announced that he was going off on a solitary journey of inland exploration. Once safely out of sight, he took advantage of the opportunity to have his spaceship land. He then made a rapid flight to the kingdom of Lonk, limiting himself to merely passing over the regions in which the crusaders were fighting to impose their religion and culture.

A few psycho-dyleptic aerosols were enough to straighten out the affairs of those groups in trouble. The local emir was subjected to a psycho-inductor treatment, and he signed a peace treaty forthwith. Tiadann was then free to rejoin his wife. Henceforth war would be banished from Noldaz. Moruns had succeeded in winning the cooperation of the Incls without oppressing them. Schools everywhere were teaching the universal language.

The only troubling matter was the continuing silence from Iern'an. The latter had given no sign since his former assistant's arrival in the New World. Was he sulking? If he was irritated, he would soon get over it. In any case, he lacked for nothing aboard his module, which was regularly resupplied by the spaceship.

And so Tiadann returned to his darling Liane on their charming hermitage near a sparkling river. She received him with a tenderness that filled her spouse's heart with joy, and they retired to their chamber, far from prying eyes. Exchanging wild kisses, they embraced passionately. Then, when their amorous ardor had been satiated, Liane, her eyes half closed, murmured gently:

"My darling, you must promise never to leave me again."

"I have no intention of leaving, my love! All I want is to spend peaceful days with you in this heavenly region. Our mission is over. But why talk like this? You know very well that I love you more than anything. . . ."

"Oh, yes, my beloved, only now you will have to love somebody else. . . ."

"What's that? What do you mean? You're not . . ."

"Yes, darling," said Liane, hiding her face in the hollow of her husband's shoulder. "I suspected it for some time, but now I'm sure. . . ."

"Good Lord! I would never have thought it possible!" exclaimed Tiadann excitedly. "That's wonderful! You're going to have to take care of yourself now! Above all, no long walks. I'm so eager to have a child by you! Tomorrow, we'll tell our friends the news. I want them to remember the day all their lives. First we'll have a banquet and invite the chief, then . . ."

Epilogue

A dazzling light invaded the room. Through the window, Liane, paralyzed with terror, saw five spheres floating over the garden at ground level. Bluish sparks of fire spouted from them and came to lick at the body of Tiadann, who in turn became luminescent.

In spite of her courage, the Lonkian heroine shrieked in horror: the skin of the man she loved seemed to burst apart and fall crackling on the ground, where it burned itself out. Then Tiadann's muscles met the same fate. Soon, all that remained was his skeleton, which seemed to be burning like branches in a hearth.

Bursting into sobs, Liane hid her face in her hands. Strange to tell, the entire phenomenon took place in a few seconds. When she raised her head again, all traces of her husband had disappeared.

Outside, six big globes were spiraling upward; they rapidly gained altitude and disappeared above the curtain of trees that grew along the river.

Liane ran from the house calling for help. The faithful Renouard appeared immediately, and she pointed out to him the minute specks of light soaring toward the clouds.

"Tiadann! Tiadann!" she moaned. "Don't leave me. . . ." Then she fainted.

Actually, there was nothing very strange about what had happened. It was simply that what the savant had feared all along had come to pass: the Galactic Inspectors had picked up his trail and were taking him back to his native planet to account for his conduct on Noldaz.

Tiadann, once more Celsar, made the trip in hermetically sealed quarters, unable to communicate with anybody. It was just as well, since he had no wish to talk; his thoughts kept ceaselessly returning to the woman he had had to abandon. There was at least one consolation: his work on Noldaz was complete. Whatever the authorities of the Imperial Lactean city did, they would be unable to disturb the reign of peace on that planet.

For this reason, when he appeared before the hierarchy of the Supreme Council he felt as frisky as a schoolboy who has just played a prank. Needless to say, Professor Iern'an was seated at the center of the tribunal. He seemed weary and aged, but his thoughts remained scrupulously concealed.

"Celsar," declared the president of this carefully chosen assembly, "you appear before us charged with serious infractions of our laws. Until now the Confederation has formally forbidden all interference in the affairs of primitives. Can you explain why you have defied our directives?"

"Oh, it's very simple, but I'm afraid you won't be able to understand me," replied the culprit. "I find it intolerable that under the pretext of noninterference we allow the developing peoples to slaughter one another! The psychological maturation of these men and women can be guided and accelerated so as to help them avoid separating into rival nations that war for pointless territorial reasons. I therefore decided to try an experiment that would show how outmoded our attitude is.

"With a common language, the peoples of Noldaz will know each other better and their territorial rivalries will be forced to an end by Lonkian power. In that way, the technological and psychological evolution of the planet will be accelerated, and war will no longer cause millions of deaths. Soon, Noldazians will be able to join our Confederation.

"For this reason I falsified the computer data: I had to give myself enough time to bring my experiment to a successful conclusion. You have managed to find me, but you must acknowledge that I have proved my point!"

"Do you really think you tricked us?" Iern'an asked in an ironic tone. "You certainly do underestimate me. . . . Happily, I have a just appreciation of *your* intellectual qualities!"

"What do you mean by that? I'm certain that no one was aware of my intentions. . . ."

"You're wrong, Celsar—I knew exactly what you were up to when you first suggested our wager!"

"What? Then why did you oppose the realization of my plans?"

"Come, now. I conveniently let myself be put out of the way of interfering, and I did nothing to keep you from doing just what you wanted to. . . ."

"So that's it! I was wondering why you hadn't been heard from."

"Yes, Celsar, that's it! A humanitarian faction of the University hoped to modify Imperial policy as it concerned underdeveloped planets. We thought that the trials of progressive maturation could be avoided along with the wars that were their corollaries. I had a certain respect for your faculties—you were a brilliant fellow—and I was aware of your thinking in this area. That's why, with the tacit permission of the Imperial government, we let you continue your experiment—and by my oath you have not disappointed me!"

"And I let myself be tricked like the worst sort of imbecile," said Celsar pitifully. "Now I understand your mocking smiles. . . ."

"Well, Celsar," continued the president of the assembly, "we must congratulate you on your magnanimous behavior and your disinterestedness. You never tried to profit from your powers. That's why the Imperial government has decided to reward you. Iern'an plans to retire and devote himself to research. You have therefore been named to the chair he occupied, and you will henceforth be able to devote yourself to the mission so dear to your heart. From now on, you will teach our students the methods to be used in accelerating the evolution of primitive planets by sparing them the trials of the normal historical cycle."

"Wonderful!" exclaimed Celsar. "I never would have aspired to such an honor. . . . But . . ."

"You are thinking of the female you married on Noldaz," the president interrupted. "It would be better if you no longer thought about her, my friend! You know that like a cut flower she will quickly fade, whereas your life has only just begun. Don't worry: she has received an oniro-suggestor treatment. Insofar as she and your friends are concerned, you died an heroic death fighting off a savage horde, and your memory will be cherished forever on Noldaz. Don't forget that the Galaxy is vast, however, and that other peoples are waiting for you."

Celsar remained silent for a moment. How could he explain to his peers that he had aspired to a pastoral existence in a world that was perhaps limited, but oh, so marvelous? And then too, he would never know his child. . . . But his scholar's temperament quickly got the upper hand. He had achieved his goal and now his duty was toward other good people who were as much to be pitied as those on Noldaz. Now that the authorities had given their agreement, he would have available to him many more highly perfected techniques.

Accepting his role, the historian then asked simply:

"What will be my next mission?"

"Fine! We have chosen the planet Druww inhabited by beings of ornithoid form. . . ."

Celsar had already forgotten Noldaz.

"I can hardly wait to consult the data stored in the central computer!" he exclaimed. "What stage of evolution are they in?"

A few days later, a spaceship took off with the new envoy of the Confederation aboard. It was headed for Druww. . . .

For a long time Iern'an followed it on the control screens. When the spaceship had disappeared, he remained thoughtful for a moment before taking up a psychic recorder and beginning to dictate the history of the pacification of Noldaz . . .

DAW sf
BOOKS